the haswell chronicles

Susey Nuttall

Web of Treason

Matador
9 De Montfort Mews
Leicester LE1 7FW, UK
Tel: (+44) 116 255 9311 / 9312
Email: books@troubador.co.uk
Web: www.troubador.co.uk/matador

ISBN 1 905237 56 1

Cover illustration: Ian Legge

Typeset in 11pt Stempel Garamond by Troubador Publishing Ltd, Leicester, UK
Printed in the UK by The Cromwell Press Ltd, Trowbridge, Wilts, UK

Matador is an imprint of Troubador Publishing Ltd

For David and Andrew.

Folio I

"When I find out which villain is responsible for this, I will make sure he receives a good whipping!"

Sir Richard Haswell stared venomously at his trembling servants. Nearby his wife, Lady Elizabeth, picked nervously at her jewelled necklace. Three of the Haswells' hunting dogs, scrawny, mangy-looking lurchers, slunk into the hall looking for scraps of food.

"And get those damnable dogs out of here!" yelled Sir Richard.

He grabbed a chair and flung it across the room. It skidded along the floor, its finely-carved legs splintering as it came to rest near the dogs, who cowered in fear.

Red-faced and scowling, Sir Richard paced up and down the line of quivering servants. Not one of them dared to raise their head and look him in the eye.

"Well?"

The question hung unanswered in the silence. No-one moved. Tom felt a tremor of fear in his legs, and he instinctively locked his knees firmly to keep himself

1

upright. Beside him, his sister Kate sniffed miserably—a mistake, for it attracted her father's attention.

"Was it you, lady?" he barked. "Messing around the stables where you shouldn't have been? Leaving doors open so my horses could escape?"

He pulled his leather gloves from his hands and flung them across the room. They slapped into a bulbous vase, ornately hand-painted in the blue and white style which was so popular with the King. It tottered violently on its base and fell to the floor, smashing as it did so. Immediately a servant rushed to sweep up the fragments, getting a snarl from Sir Richard for his troubles.

"Four of my finest horses, bought at a cost of 60 royals each, disappeared! Gone! Of course, I can replace them at some expense—but that's not the point, is it?"

He paused and glowered at the assembled household, his eyes boring like gimlets into their pale, blank faces. Tom hastily averted his eyes and made an intense study of the floor. Experience had taught him it was wise to adopt a low profile.

"The point," his father continued, "is that someone here is careless with my property. And not for the first time either. Last month it was a fire in one of my barns. All the winter's hay went up in flames and it was damn lucky no-one was killed—all because someone knocked a lamp over. Someone does not appreciate my generosity in giving them employment, and a damn fine roof over their heads. Have I not rewarded you for your work? Given you the privilege of working on the Haswell estates?

Lower Myersford Hall is one of the finest houses in Lancashire—and this is how you repay me!"

"My lord Haswell, if I may speak a word in private?"

Tom looked up to see his father's accountant, Sir Jacob Carew, standing by the doorway. His pinched white face contrasted vividly with his richly embroidered red and gold doublet. Sir Richard glared once more at the quaking servant who was frantically sweeping up shards of pottery and splinters of wood, and stalked over to the doorway.

"What?" At Sir Richard's sharp tone, the accountant winced momentarily.

He swallowed hard before replying. Tom watched him closely, hoping to catch a snippet of the conversation. Anything that got someone else into trouble was worth knowing, he thought. Particularly if it's that slug, Carew.

"Wiswall, the Constable, reports that four horses have been found wandering the estate at Langford, up by the Priory, my lord. From his description, it seems that they are your missing horses."

"The Priory, eh? So it's these Papists again. The King's right about them—troublemakers, the lot of them. If I had it in my power…"

"We don't know for certain it's…er…Papists," Sir Jacob went on. "It could just be as we thought, accidental—carelessness. Someone left the stable door open perhaps. Not deliberate at all…"

Sir Richard cut him short and turned to walk back along the line of servants. Tom knew what was coming next. Every time the word 'papist' was mentioned, it was the same old lecture. He stared down at his father's polished riding boots which stopped right in front of him. His heart quickened its pace and his mouth was suddenly dry.

"Papists, hmm? I hope you've not been trying to contact Fishwyck again. Have you?"

"No, sir."

Tom's voice cracked as he replied and his lips stuck to his teeth. He swallowed hard before continuing. "I haven't seen him since they left."

Out of the corner of his eye, he saw Carew's smirk of triumph.

"Good." Sir Richard inhaled slowly. "Let's keep it that way. The Fishwycks are fools, every one of them, and they follow the ways of Rome. In this house we are loyal to the King and attend his new Church."

At his father's words, a sudden hot flash of anger coursed through Tom's veins. How could his father say that? Edward Fishwyck was certainly no fool!

Sir Richard swung round and once more faced his silent household.

"And that goes for all of you as well. We worship in an English Church, not a Papist den of idols and fake relics. To do otherwise is to defy the King's order. That's treason—and you know the fate of traitors."

"My lord, I'm sure none here is a traitor."

Lady Elizabeth's gentle voice broke the tension, and Sir Richard looked fixedly at his wife, his eyes like glowing embers in a dying fire.

"Sure? You'd better be sure. There's a gallows waiting at Lancaster for those who plot rebellion and treason. Now, in the Name of all that is Holy, will someone get me my riding cloak and gloves? I have four horses to bring back from Langford. Sir Jacob, you stay here and find who's responsible. Middlemore, the groom, can escort me. And get those accounts ready for me—I want to check them again."

Sir Richard spun round and strode out of the room, slamming the door behind him. Its echoes reverberated for a few seconds and then it seemed as if the whole house heaved a collective sigh of relief.

Lady Elizabeth was the first to break the silence. Her voice quavered but she spoke with authority.

"Everyone to your duties. We have a house to run here. Sir Richard won't be back until sunset and he'll expect a good meal."

Immediately, the servants scattered, leaving Tom and Kate alone in the room with their mother. Tom noticed for the first time his mother's tired eyes and pale lips, and wondered if she was ill. She smiled wearily at them.

"Go off and play somewhere for what's left of the afternoon—but not near the stables. You know your father doesn't want you disturbing the horses. And be back in time for supper."

A grim silence descended over the children as they walked out of the Hall and set off towards the rose arbour. Nearby, a family of ducks waddled across the neatly trimmed lawn, occasionally snapping at an inviting tuft of grass. The summer sunshine was warm and bright, the sky a blue canopy with delicate wisps of clouds like grey mares' tails. Tom glanced up; there was perhaps an hour of daylight left.

"Why did you lie, Tom?" Kate looked up at her older brother, her eyes clouded with puzzlement.

"I didn't lie. What did I say that was a lie?"

"You said you hadn't seen Edward Fishwyck."

Tom sat down on a low wall and frowned at her. "I haven't seen him. You know that."

"But you tried to," persisted Kate as she sat down beside him. "You even climbed the walls of their estate to see if you could find him."

"Ah, but I didn't see him, did I? So I didn't lie. Father didn't ask me if I'd *tried* to see him. It's not the same thing."

Kate nodded, but Tom wasn't sure that she really understood. How could he explain, in words a nine-year-old would understand, what problems the King's divorce from Queen Catherine had brought? How people were forced to choose between obedience to the King and allegiance to Rome? He ran his hands through his short-cropped, brown hair, as if to stimulate his thoughts.

"Edward was a good friend and I really miss him being here. But his family stayed loyal to Rome."

He paused, remembering the day when his father told him he and Edward couldn't play together any more.

"You know how keen Father is to keep the Hall and

its estates. And that takes a lot of hard work and money. Since the King set up his own church, we have to be careful. If we don't do what the King wants, he'll send in his commissioners to take it from us, just like he did with the Fishwycks."

Kate was silent for a moment. A plaintive note crept into her voice. "I don't want to leave Myersford. I really like it here. It's much bigger than the old place."

"So do I," agreed Tom. "But that's how it is these days. The King gave us the house, but he could just as easily take it back—like he did with the people who lived here before us."

"But it was a reward! Father helped find those plotters three years ago. Surely the King wouldn't take it back again?"

Kate's voice was shrill with indignation.

Tom thought for a moment. Kate was right. The old place was much smaller than Myersford. Comfortable enough, but Myersford was much more, well, *fun*. There were more spaces to hide in, more land to run in. But no friends anywhere nearby. And the King could do anything he pleased—as his father never tired of reminding him.

A cool breeze wafted through the apple trees above them, and Tom shivered involuntarily. He looked up and saw the dark, golden sun low in the sky. Nightfall wasn't far away and his father would be home soon. A low growl from his stomach confirmed what Tom already suspected—it was nearly supper time.

"Hell's teeth, I'm hungry," announced Tom, using an oath he had heard his father use.

Kate tutted, her lips pursed in a pink rosebud of disapproval.

"Stop trying to be so grown up, Tom. It's not nice. Now let's go."

"Listen to you, Mistress Priss," he shot back.

He turned and ran off in the direction of the Hall, chased by a furious Kate. With luck, supper would be waiting for them. Their route home took them through the knot garden and round the back of the stables. As they rounded the corner, Tom suddenly caught sight of four men deep in conversation by the stable door.

"Who are they?" Kate voiced his thoughts exactly, and he shook his head in response.

He was about to turn away, thinking to alert someone at the Hall of the men's presence when he realised with a jolt that one of them was Carew.

That's strange, he thought. What's he doing round the stables? He usually stays well away from there. Too dirty and smelly for his liking. He motioned Kate to stay back and stepped forward slowly.

Carew was the only one talking, gesturing wildly with his hands. Even from this distance, Tom could see his pale, angry face. But who was he talking to? Tom couldn't recognise them at all. Certainly no-one who'd visited the house recently. He inched forward again, but carelessly, for his boot dislodged a stone.

"Damn!" he muttered angrily, as the clatter reached

the ears of Carew and his friends. They all turned to look in Tom's direction. Quickly, he darted behind a nearby rhododendron bush, hoping that they hadn't seen him. Holding his breath and listening for approaching footsteps, he stayed motionless. No-one came. After a minute or so, he felt brave enough to peer round the bush. But there was no-one there.

He rejoined Kate who wanted to know what he'd seen.

"Nothing much," he whispered to Kate. "And if we're found, we'll be in trouble. We'd better get back for supper, otherwise Father will be there before us and will want to know where we've been."

Kate nodded, and they crept back behind the low box hedge and made their way briskly back to the Hall. But Tom was troubled. In all the time that Carew had worked for his father, Tom had never known him go anywhere near the stables. In fact, Carew professed to be allergic to horses; he said they made him sneeze. So why was he there? And who were the men who were with him?

Folio II

Tom lay awake in his bed-chamber, gazing at the walls. His mind was alert, full of the day's strange events, and he was a long way from sleep. It was a warm and stuffy night. A nocturnal insect had intruded into the room and irritated Tom with its sleepy buzzing. Narrow shafts of moonlight arrowed their way through the open window and bathed the room in a pale glow. Tom tried squinting his eyes in such a way that some of the dappled patterns on the ceiling started to look like people's faces. One of them looked reassuringly like his mother, put there to watch over him as he slept.

Supper was uneventful, except that his father did not join them as usual. He was still not back from collecting the horses and, according to his mother, the culprit had been punished. That's something of a relief, thought Tom. At least we know the horses weren't stolen. And it will teach them to be more careful in future.

His thoughts turned to the men with Carew that he'd seen earlier by the stables. Maybe they had something to do with it? Of course, it could be that they were new neighbours, noblemen or wealthy merchants who had recently been given their lands by the King. Sometimes it was wise not to enquire too deeply into the appearance of new faces and the disappearance of familiar ones. Despite his youth, Tom had heard enough of adult discussion (or more accurately, overheard) to know that King Henry was a harsh judge of men, but to be favoured by him held rich rewards.

The idea of them being new neighbours made Tom think once more of his old friend, Edward Fishwyck and the time when they stayed up all night. It was the Christmas feast two years earlier, and Edward was allowed to stay at Myersford. It was Edward who'd taught him how to climb out of the bedroom window. He'd escaped a punishment that time. He smiled as he remembered how they hadn't been able to climb back again. Not only was Edward a good friend, but his father also was a regular visitor to the Hall. Round, red-faced and jovial, he always had a cheery word of greeting for Tom. But Edward and his family suddenly stopped visiting, creating an emptiness in Tom's life. And when he rode past the Fishwyck estate one day with his father, he felt his stomach start to churn, for the gates were barred and the house empty. Soon after, a rich London merchant moved into the house with his family and servants, and Sir Richard made Tom promise never to see Edward again.

That's one promise I've only just managed to keep, he thought in annoyance.

He tried to contact Edward—left messages for him by the wall where the Haswell estate met the Fishwyck lands —but the only person who read them was Carew—who promptly informed Sir Richard, and the inevitable beating followed.

Tom turned over several times, trying to find a cool patch of bedding. The humid night air was hot and oppressive, and Tom felt the heavy sheets clinging to his legs. He threw back the covers and thrust his legs out impatiently. Then he sat up, plumped up his pillows and flopped down again. Why was it that when you were really tired, you could never get to sleep?

Tom's frustration turned suddenly to unease, as a noise outside disturbed his thoughts. Lying completely still, and holding his breath, Tom listened. What was that noise? And where was it coming from? There it was again; outside, he was sure of that, close to the house, on the gravel—a crunching sound, as if something, or someone, was walking carefully, trying not to be heard. Then it stopped, and was replaced by a soft swishing noise. Tom knew at once where the sound was coming from; it was a shortcut that he'd used many times to sneak back into the house unnoticed. The narrow strip of grass that lay alongside the path led straight to the servants' entrance.

Tom slipped from his bed and padded softly to the window. He felt the panelled wooden floor cold against his bare feet, making him shiver momentarily. Peering out carefully, so as not to be seen, Tom hoped to catch a glimpse of the visitor. Who was it? Inside his chest, his heart began to beat a little faster.

Craning his neck, Tom leaned nearer to the open window. It was a bright moonlit night, and he could easily make out the roof of the stable block. The sharply defined lines of boxwood that made up the knot garden were clearly visible. The orderly rows of fruit-trees in the orchard barely moved in the night air. A tiny spider was spinning its delicate web across the casement, strand by fragile strand. But of the mysterious visitor, Tom could see nothing.

Suddenly, the moon sailed behind a cloud, and the landscape was suddenly dark and indistinct. That was definitely a person, thought Tom. The footsteps are too light for a horse. Smaller animals are much quieter.

Then, as abruptly as it had disappeared, the moonlight returned, and Tom once more had a clear view. He stared intently into the distance, hoping his eyes would recognise a dark shape in the even darker shadows, but all in vain. He could make out nothing that looked like the mysterious prowler. He did catch sight of a small animal scampering across the lawns—probably a rabbit or a small fox—but nothing else.

Tom waited a few minutes, savouring the warm, exciting feeling of spying unobserved from the window. In the distance, the church bell chimed the hour. He was just about to turn and climb back into his bed, when a quiet creaking caused him to stop and listen once more. That sounded like the servants' door. It always creaked like that. Surely it wasn't his father returning so late? No, he wouldn't use the servants' entrance anyway. Perhaps it was Master Hollindrake? Tom snorted as he remembered how the tutor spent much of his free time in the company of the servants—the young, female servants.

Moving on tiptoe now, Tom headed towards the door of his bed-chamber. He could hear soft footsteps coming along the corridor. Ignoring the pounding in his chest, he opened the door a crack—just enough to see someone creep past. There was a momentary flash of red and gold and then the night-time prowler was gone. But it was enough for Tom to know his identity. There was only one man who wore red and gold—Carew. What's he doing up at this time, sneaking around the servants' entrance? he wondered. He's usually the first to retire. And what business does he have that takes him outside at night?

Folio III

Despite the disturbances of the night, Tom awoke refreshed the following morning. His first thoughts were of Carew and his night-time exploits. Maybe he was visiting one of the kitchen maids? As he looked out of his bed-chamber window, a smile came to Tom's lips. Here was a good chance to get Carew in trouble, for a change.

"Let's see how he likes having tales told about him," he said to his reflection in the glass. Then he turned and scampered downstairs.

Breakfast was the usual fare of milk, bread and cheese, and Kate and his parents were already at the table. With a twinge of annoyance, he saw that Carew was also in the room, shuffling some papers.

"Good morning, Father," he said brightly, and shook his father's hand. "Good morning, Mother."

Lady Elizabeth turned her face towards him and offered her cheek for his usual kiss. Tom noticed with relief that her paleness of the previous day had now gone. He took his seat and waited for one of his parents to ask how he'd slept. But neither Sir Richard nor Lady Elizabeth was particularly talkative, and the meal continued in silence. Kate, too, stayed silent, and Tom wondered if he'd missed something. Was his father still angry and no-one would speak, fearing his temper would be provoked once more?

He glanced quickly at his father's finely chiselled face and decided to make the first move.

"Did you sleep well, Mother? You looked tired yesterday."

"I slept very well, thank you, Thomas."

His mother looked at him curiously, then resumed eating. Tom tried again.

"And you, Father? How did you sleep?"

His father glared at him.

"That's a damn fool question, isn't it? How did I sleep? Well, after a journey of several miles to retrieve four horses that some idle peasant let loose, how do you think I slept?"

Tom was silent for a few minutes. He looked at Kate. Ask me, his eyes pleaded. Ask me how *I* slept. But Kate didn't ask him. He decided to try one final time.

"I didn't sleep at all well," he announced, to no-one in particular. "I was awake for almost the whole night."

Behind him the noise of papers being rapidly shuffled told him that his opening shot had hit home.

"In fact," he continued, "I'm sure there was someone prowling around outside. I'm positive I heard footsteps. Maybe we should check to make sure nothing's been stolen?"

There was a loud bang, and they all turned round to see Carew picking up a large heavy book and a sheaf of papers from the floor. His hard green eyes met Tom's for a few seconds.

"My apologies, my lord. The mention of burglars is very worrying...perhaps the horses..." he stuttered.

"I doubt it," Sir Richard said, dismissively. "But tell Middlemore to keep an eye on things and to check the stables anyway."

Carew bowed and continued to shuffle his papers.

"You haven't seen my gold chain, have you, Sir Jacob? The one that Sir Richard brought me from the Low Countries?" Lady Elizabeth asked.

She ran her fingers gently along the neckline of her damask gown.

"I haven't seen it for some time now. I know I had it when we held the Easter feast, but I can't find it now."

There was a pause, and then Carew spoke.

"No, my lady. I haven't seen it anywhere. Would you like me to search the servants' quarters? Perhaps..."

"A good idea, Carew. But not today. Lady Elizabeth has probably put it somewhere and forgotten where. "

"As you wish, my lord. But I really do feel we should be cautious. We've already had a fire and then the horses escaped. If there is someone here who shouldn't be—a sneakthief, or worse—maybe the children should stay near the Hall. I'm sure I saw you down by the stables yesterday morning, Master Thomas, just before we discovered that the horses were missing."

Tom looked at Carew. He was smiling amiably, but Tom noticed that the smile didn't reach the icy green coldness of his eyes.

"Is that true, Thomas? Were you by the stables?" Sir Richard's tone was sharp.

Tom burned with silent anger. He should have known this would happen. Instead of being in trouble himself, Carew had neatly turned the tables on him. But this time he had his answer ready.

"Yes, Father. I *was* by the stables, but it was much later, closer to evening. Yesterday morning I was in my lessons with Master Hollindrake."

Sir Richard stared at Tom, as if he couldn't make up his mind whether to believe him or not. Then he said, "Very well. But from now on, stay away from the stables. At thirteen years of age, you should be able to follow simple instructions."

"Yes, Father."

The meal continued in silence until everyone had finished eating. At Sir Richard's command, a servant rushed to clear to table.

Outside, the early morning sunshine beckoned, but first there was work to do. Kate headed in the direction of the small schoolroom where she sat with her mother. Tom settled himself for his morning's study in the main schoolroom with his tutor, Master Hollindrake.

Writing and Drawing was one of his favourite subjects and he was currently working on a series of sketches showing the various buildings of the estate. He added the finishing touches to his drawing of the knot garden and put his drawing quill down. 'How can I visit the stables without defying Father?' he wondered. His eyes drifted to the sketch in front of him and he stared idly at the black ink-lines, still wet and glossy. That's it! he thought. That's the answer!

He raised his head and turned to his tutor. Casually, he asked, "Master Hollindrake, I'd like to start on a sketch of the stable block next. Can we go over there and work outside?"

Master Hollindrake considered this for a moment and then said, "No, Master Thomas. I don't think that will be possible today. But later in the week, we could consider it."

"Why not today?" persisted Tom.

"Because your father wants no more disturbances around the estate. He's expecting visitors—some friends of Sir Jacob Carew—and there is a lot of work to be done to make ready for them."

Tom's ears pricked up. This was news indeed! Visitors usually meant a banquet—and that meant he could stay up late. Maybe Kate would know more about it?

But when he asked her in the orchard that afternoon, Kate could tell him no more.

"Visitors? Friends of Sir Jacob?" she asked.

"Yes."

Kate swung gently on a rope-swing, her full skirts blowing back as she did so. She looked up at Tom who was standing on a makeshift rope-bridge.

"Mother didn't mention anything about visitors. Do you think they'll stay long? I can't see her missing a chance to put on a feast. You know how she loves to entertain guests," she said. "But she did say that they knew who had left the stable door open."

"Did she say who?" asked Tom.

"No. Just that they knew who it was."

A fragrant haze rose from the lavender bushes that hedged the orchard, and even from his vantage point high on the rope-bridge, Tom could pick out the black and yellow of the bumble bees hovering between the small lilac stalks. He gazed pensively into the distance and set his jaw firmly. The visit to the stables might have been thwarted the previous day, but today it would be different—even if I have to risk a beating, he decided.

"Let's try the stables again," he said, suddenly.

"But Father said we had to stay away from there."

"I know," Tom grinned back. "That's why I want to go there. Come on, it won't take long. If we're careful and avoid the paths, no-one will see us."

Kate hesitated a moment, then jumped off the rope-swing and smoothed down her skirt. Tom was already racing ahead and Kate had to run to catch him up. By taking a short cut through the rose arbour, a route which brought them to the rear of the stable block, they arrived breathless but unseen close to the old stalls. Silently they crept into the stables and edged their way round to the storage stalls.

The strong, pungent smell of horses, mingled with the

rich odour of fine quality leather, drifted towards Tom and he breathed in deeply. It was a warm, comforting place, full of straw and animal foods, and today it was spiced with the excitement of a forbidden visit.

As they stared round the stall, Tom had the uneasy feeling that they were not alone. They couldn't see anyone, and there was nothing to show that anyone was there, but he felt suddenly uncomfortable, as if they were being watched. The warm pleasure of a moment earlier evaporated in an instant. Kate shuffled her feet impatiently, and was about to speak when Tom motioned her to keep quiet. He listened carefully.

"What are you doing?" she whispered.

"I thought I heard something," replied Tom, quietly.

"It was probably a field-mouse," said Kate, unconcerned.

"No, listen," he continued, and both children held their breath and stood motionless, straining their ears for the slightest sound.

Nothing. Tom was about to speak when suddenly he heard it—a soft, rustling noise. He looked at Kate, and knew from her wide, scared eyes that she had heard it too. They stood motionless, afraid even to run away, and listened again, hoping vainly that they had both imagined it.

There it was again, as if something was moving in the straw, something much larger than a field-mouse. It was coming from the corner of the furthest stall where there was a mound of straw piled up against the wall.

Tom walked slowly over to the mound and stood a foot away. Reaching out, he found a rusty pitch-fork leaning against the wall and with the handle he prodded cautiously at the mound. He felt the handle meet a solid object under the mound, and then the mound moved! With his heart racing wildly, and his legs trembling, Tom prodded again.

This time the mound cried out and moved away a little. The straw fell away and Tom could see that it was a person, a child—although it looked more like a bundle of rags.

"It's Mary!" cried Kate, in a shocked voice.

Tom looked closer, and then realised who was lying in front of him. It was Mary Palmer, one of the kitchen maids, but she looked nothing like the Mary he remembered. For instead of the smiling face and bright eyes of the Mary who helped in the kitchens, and sat with the rest of the servants in church, he saw a bedraggled, bruised and blood-stained girl, just a little older than himself, terrified beyond words.

Folio IV

Tom and Kate stared, horrified. Mary was cowering, trembling with fear, in a corner of the stall. Her coarse woollen dress was torn and bloodstained, and her face was bruised and bloody. One eye was turning purple, and it was so swollen that it was almost closed. Dried blood matted her fair hair, and along her bare arms and legs were harsh red weals.

"God's Blood!" blurted out Tom. He quickly removed his jacket and laid it gently over Mary.

Tears filled Kate's eyes and she knelt down impulsively to comfort Mary.

"What's happened? Who did this?" she asked in a hushed voice.

Mary shifted slowly and painfully into a sitting position. Her face was dirty, and pale streaks revealed where the tears had run.

Quietly, she replied, "Sir Jacob Carew."

"Carew? Why?" Tom couldn't imagine Carew laying a hand to anyone. It's more his style to get someone else to do his dirty work, he thought grimly.

"He said I let the horses go free—but I didn't!" she replied, suddenly angry. "I were nowhere near the stables that day. Please believe me, it weren't me!"

"So why did he say it was you?" asked Kate.

Mary was suddenly quiet again, and seemed almost reluctant to talk. She looked at Kate again and then said, "You wouldn't understand. You're one of 'em."

"One of who?" asked Tom. "Tell us so we *can* understand."

Almost sullenly, Mary replied, "You're rich. You have a real nice house, fine clothes, good food. You don't have to work in the kitchen like I do. You have toys and books—and can come here whenever you like and ride the horses."

She paused and stared resentfully at them.

"When you're just a servant like I am, you're nowt. You're just a nobody who don't matter."

Tom sat down in the straw beside the two girls and tried to imagine his life without the things Mary mentioned. He couldn't. Mary was right; he had no idea what it would be like if he had to work, or live in a small house like Mary and her family, with just one room and no windows.

Mary sniffed and continued her tale.

"Sometimes, when I've finished in the kitchen, I come down here to see the horses. When I talk to 'em, it's almost like they understand all I say. And sometimes I help Mr Middlemore groom 'em, until their coats go all shiny."

She eyed Tom warily, sniffed loudly again, and drew her hand roughly across her face.

"Sir Jacob told my mam that I must have left the door open so the horses got out, but I didn't. I weren't here the day they went missing. I were in the kitchens all day. And what's more Sir Jacob knows that because he saw me there. But he's one of you as well, and no-one would believe me."

Tom had to admit, she had a point. He'd been on the receiving end of Carew's mischief-making more times than once. And if it's ever a case of Carew's word against mine, he thought bitterly, Carew always wins.

Mary eased herself gently into a more comfortable position. As she did so, Tom's coat fell from her body. Tom could now see that hardly a part of her body was untouched. Kate's eyes widened in horror.

"I'll get some water and wash those...er... for you," she offered, and taking a small pail, she set off.

When she returned, she also had a small piece of grey-white cloth with her. Gently, she washed Mary's wounds, removing the dirt and cleaning the open cuts. Mary's eyes thanked her silently, then she said, "You won't tell anyone I'm here, will you? I've nowhere else to go and Sir Jacob thinks I've left the Hall."

Tom screwed up his eyes and looked at her.

"Can't you go back to your family?"

Mary shook her head, and Tom watched as a tear trickled silently down her face. What could have upset her so much? He wished he hadn't asked.

"Not really. Sir Jacob told 'em to leave, all of 'em. And with no work, there's no money. They've moved over the valley, but I have to stay—I can't walk with these."

She indicated the swollen red wounds on her legs. Tom turned away; he could almost feel her pain.

Kate looked at Tom, her eyes pleading with him. After a second's hesitation, Tom said, "We won't tell anyone, promise." Then a thought struck him. "Have you eaten anything?" he asked.

"No, not since yesterday morning," said Mary.

"Then we'll bring you some food—this evening, after supper. Between us we should be able to get something for you. And I think there may be some raspberries near the kitchen. You could sneak up when no-one's looking," suggested Tom.

For a moment, Mary looked worried.

"What's the matter?" asked Tom.

Mary sighed. "I tried that last night—sneaking out when everyone were asleep—or so I thought. But there were people about, and I were afraid I would be seen. And I couldn't walk very far anyway. I saw at least three people out last night besides me. One of 'em were Sir Jacob, I'm certain of that. But there were others as well."

"So I was right!" exclaimed Tom. "It *was* Carew I saw sneaking back into the Hall last night."

Kate looked at her brother in bewilderment.

"What are you talking about? You said this morning you'd heard a prowler last night. You didn't say anything about seeing Sir Jacob."

"I know—but I couldn't very well say that with Carew there, could I? And Father didn't seem all that bothered anyway. He just said we had to stay away from the stables."

"So what are you doing here then?" Mary asked.

Tom thought for a moment and then said, "I saw Carew here yesterday, talking to someone I didn't know. He usually stays well away from the stables. Might spoil his clothes. I wondered what was so interesting. Have you seen him here?"

Mary shook her head. "No, I've not seen Carew, but I did once think that there were someone in the bushes outside."

"Maybe it was an animal?" suggested Kate.

"Probably," said Mary. "But it give me a fright. I don't like going outside at night now. Especially since I saw Sir Jacob and the others. If they found me..."

Her voice trailed off. There was no need to say any more.

All the night-time activity puzzled Tom, but also worried him. The stables might not be such a safe place for Mary to stay. He said as much to Kate on the way back to the Hall.

Kate screwed up her eyes, and twisted the damp cloth between her hands.

"Mary doesn't deserve to be beaten and thrown out of her home. It's just not fair and I think we should take care of her. Is there anywhere else we can hide her?" she asked.

"We'll have to see. Let's get some food for her first,"

replied Tom. "By the way, where did you get that cloth?"

Kate looked down at the scrap of woollen fabric in her hands.

"I found it caught on one of the large thorny bushes near the stables," she said.

Tom took it and looked at it closely. It was a coarsely woven material, which had stitching and loose threads down one side of it, almost like a pocket that had been torn off.

"I wonder where this came from?" he thought aloud. "It doesn't look like any material I've seen before."

Kate shrugged her shoulders. "It came in useful though," she said. "Come on, let's see what we can get for Mary."

Within a few minutes, they were by the gravel path that led to the servants' entrance. Tom took a quick look round. Good, he thought. No-one's around.

"Quick! Stay off the path in case we make a noise on the gravel," he hissed to Kate. "And head for the pantry. There should be something we can take for Mary."

Seconds later, they reached the door. Taking care not to let it creak, Tom opened it just wide enough for him to slip through.

"You stay here and keep watch," he ordered.

The pantry was lined with shelves, all laden with preserved fruits for the winter, salted fish and sacks of grain. Tom breathed in, savouring the musty, spiced atmosphere and his mouth watered hungrily. In front of him, on the lowest shelf was a loaf, still warm from the oven, and a small hunk of cheese. He grabbed them and stuffed them into his pockets — but not before giving in to the warm tempting smell of the freshly-baked bread.

"Tom!" Kate's urgent whisper echoed through the crack in the door. "Come quick!"

Hurriedly, Tom squeezed back out through the door and rejoined his sister.

"What is it?" he gasped.

But his question met with silence. Kate was staring ashen-faced down the main pathway to the entrance to the Hall. Tom followed her gaze. He could scarcely believe what he saw. His heart increased its pace, and he felt the panic rise into his throat. For clustered around the steps to the main entrance were several heavily armed men on horseback.

Folio V

Tom felt an urge to cry out, to warn his family. The words died on his lips, as one of the men dismounted and stepped up to the main entrance. He raised his hand and hammered violently on the huge wooden door.

"Open in the King's name!" he shouted. "We have a Justice's Warrant to search your property!"

A Justice's Warrant? What could they hope to find? Tom's mind spun in panic. Unseen hands drew back the bolts with a thud and the men, now all dismounted and with swords drawn, rushed into the Hall. Tom turned to Kate and pushed her roughly into a large rhododendron bush.

"Don't move!" His voice was hoarse and dry. "Don't come into the Hall until I call you!"

He turned quickly and sprinted round to the servants' entrance. Good! The door was still open. He slipped in and felt his way silently along the dark narrow corridor, past the pantry. Overhead, the constant thud of boots revealed the extent of the search. Tom could feel the rushing blood pounding in his ears, and his breathing came in shallow bursts. As he crept along using the decorative wall panels to guide him, his hand touched an ornate wall carving. He paused to regain his breath and leaned heavily on the panelled wall. Suddenly it gave way and he tumbled backwards.

"What on earth…?"

He peered into the darkness, hoping for a light to guide his way. But there was none, only an enveloping gloom. Where was he? It looked like some kind of tunnel, but where did it go?

He got to his feet and moved forward gingerly, reaching out sideways with his hands to touch the roughly hewn stonework of the walls. Delicate strands of cobwebs trailed down from the low roof and clung to his hair. What was this place? A secret passageway that no-one knew about? This was a great find! He smiled as he imagined all the tricks he could play on Kate.

"Ow! Damn it!"

A lightning pain shot through his leg as his shin made contact with a solid object on the ground. As he fumbled around in the half-gloom, his hands touched something rough and wooden. A box? Then he felt another—and another. A shaft of disappointment—someone already knew about the passageway and was using it just to store boxes.

Tom clambered over them and continued his exploration. Through the wall, he could still hear the sounds of the search. "So whatever they're looking for," he muttered, "they haven't found it."

Abruptly, the passageway came to an end. The wall was no longer on his right hand side, but directly in front of him.

"There must be a way out," he murmured. "Maybe there's a lever or something to press."

He ran his hands slowly over the wall in front of him. Nothing. He tapped carefully on the wall. Again, nothing. It sounded solid and firm.

"Let's try the other side then," he said aloud. The air was rank and fetid, and a rising fear played along Tom's sinews.

At the back of his mind the unspoken horror lurked; what if I can't find a way out? What if I'm trapped here for ever...? Don't be stupid, he told himself—you can always shout or bang on the wall, or go back the way you came.

His hands touched the stone wall on the left hand side and he repeated the process of tapping gently. This wall seemed perfectly solid too, until he no longer felt the wall, but a small wooden panel, low down near the ground.

Tom's shaking hands searched for a way to push the panel, or pull it out. It seems loose, he thought, so it must move. Frantically, he worked at the panel, willing it to move. Then his fingers touched a small knob. Taking a firm hold, he pulled hard. It worked! The panel shot sideways, leaving a small hole. Tom stuck his head out, blinking rapidly in the bright light and gulping the fresh air.

As his eyes grew accustomed to the unfamiliar

brilliance of the daylight, he saw that he was in his father's study. It was deserted, but the scattered papers and open drawers told of a thorough search.

Tom squeezed out carefully and replaced the panel. Running now, he followed the shouts of men, and the thud of heavy boots on the oak panelled floor mirrored the beating of his heart.

As he skidded to a halt on the polished floor of the Great Hall, he saw several burly men, armed with fearsome swords, rummaging through cupboards and peering behind tapestries. He ran to his mother, who turned and clung to him, her anxious fingers gouging into his shoulders.

"Oh, Tom! Thank the good Lord you're safe!" Her eyes were wide and staring, her lips pinched and pale. Then, "Where's Kate? Where is she?" Lady Elizabeth almost screamed at him.

"Hiding outside," he replied. His words reassured his mother, for she released her grip on him a little, although she kept hold of him.

Tom's attention was held by the men; heart in mouth, he wondered what they wanted. Maybe there had been a mistake? Why would they need to search the Hall? Around the room, the servants were clustered in small whispering groups. He watched as his father walked quickly down the stairs and spoke calmly to one of the men who was standing quietly to one side—a tall, wiry man with grey, thinning hair and craggy features. There was something familiar about him, although Tom was sure he didn't know him. Something in his bearing, his way of standing—where had he seen him before?

"Who's the man with Father?" he whispered to Lady Elizabeth.

"The Sheriff, Sir Charles Gerard. Why do you ask?"

Tom shook his head. "Oh, no reason."

The Sheriff went to stand at the bottom of the great staircase and stamped his foot hard on the bottom stair. When the chattering of the servants ceased and a respectful silence descended, he spoke. His booming voice resounded in the vaulted ceiling of the Hall.

"One of the White Monks of Langford, a heretic priest, has been seen in this area."

In the silence that followed, no-one moved. Sir Charles scanned each face carefully, his eyes challenging the fearful household.

"This man is a known rebel, a traitor, and loyal subjects have told me that he is plotting evil deeds. Deeds which will make your blood turn to ice."

He paused again. Tom held his breath. Surely there was no plot at Myersford?

The Sheriff continued, "This rebel, this so-called man of God, intends to kill the King, God's Chosen One, and replace him with the Papist Princess Mary."

A sharp gasp of horror swelled in the corners of the room. Who would plot do such a thing? Kill the King?

"There is no Papist here, my Lord." Sir Richard's firm and reassuring voice silenced the watching servants. "This is a loyal house."

"Nevertheless, you know the penalty for treason. There are those who still continue with the Old Religion in secret, aided by such priests, who roam the country, inciting rebellion."

Sir Charles glared at the assembled household. His gaze fell on Tom, and for a second Tom almost looked away. But he didn't. His eyes met the Sheriff's defiantly and held them, and it was Sir Charles who looked away first.

Tom thought about the people he knew. They all went to church, and listened intently for what seemed like an eternity. Of course, you didn't have a choice; there were punishments if you didn't attend, but surely none of these people would harbour a priest on the run when they knew the penalty was death?

The sound of boots echoing through the Hall increasingly loudly indicated that the men had completed their search. The genial conversation between the Sheriff and Sir Richard suggested that all was well.

Sir Charles turned to go and strode briskly to the main door. His men followed him and in less than a minute, they were indistinct shapes in the distance surrounded by a cloud of dust kicked up by the horses' hooves. But at the back of Tom's mind something nagged at him, a vague feeling of unease, like a sugar-blackened tooth before it erupted into toothache.

Sir Richard walked over to Tom and his mother who, despite the July evening warmth, was trembling. He put his arm around her shoulder and ruffled Tom's hair.

"We have nothing to hide, and nothing to worry about. Sir Charles has a job to do. As a Justice of the Peace, he must pursue all traitors. He is a good man, you know."

He turned to Tom.

"Where's your sister?"

"Hiding outside. She's safe. I made sure of that."

Sir Richard nodded his head in the direction of the gardens.

"You'd better find her then. Let her know all is well here."

Tom bowed respectfully to his father and scurried off to the kitchen corridor. He went straight to the exposed entrance and quickly replaced the panel. Even from close up, it was impossible to tell there was a secret passageway there. It's really quite ingenious, he thought. I wonder why it was built?

Picking his way carefully through the evening shadows of the vegetable garden, he made his way back to where he'd left Kate.

"Kate?" he called, into the rhododendron bush. "Kate, are you there?"

There was no reply, but a rustling of leaves nearby caused him to turn round quickly—just in time to see Kate emerging, dishevelled and grubby, her fair hair adorned with purple petals and leaf-tips.

"What happened, Tom?"

She clung fiercely to his arm and shook him.

"Tell me—what happened?"

"It was the Sheriff, looking for a priest from the Priory. Father doesn't seem concerned about it. They think it's a plot to kill King Henry and put Princess Mary on the throne instead."

"You mean Queen Anne's daughter? But she's younger than me!" Kate's face showed her puzzlement.

"No," replied Tom. "Queen Catherine's daughter. The Catholic one."

Tom smirked, enjoying the superiority this snippet of knowledge gave him.

"And I thought all the monks had left Langford when it was closed down?"

Kate screwed up her face and looked at Tom. A sudden cool wind caught her hair and blew a strand across her face. Tom reached out and moved it back into place. Gently, he picked off a large spider that was crawling just above her ear and flicked it into the bushes.

"They have," he said, "but they've got to go somewhere, I suppose."

She relaxed her hold on his arm.

"So everyone's safe? Mother and Father?"

Tom hesitated a moment. Somewhere a wood-pigeon called out repeatedly, breaking the silence. He looked up through the leaves and branches of the nearby trees at the summer sky. Small white clouds were beginning to form in the west.

"Flocks of sheep," he murmured at last. "It'll rain tomorrow."

Kate tugged insistently at his arm. "You haven't

answered my question—everyone's safe, aren't they?"

Tom nodded.

"For the moment, yes."

"And the Sheriff will catch the priest and punish him, won't he?"

Again, he hesitated. The vague uneasiness suddenly crystallised into serious doubt; for he remembered, with absolute clarity the figures he'd seen with Carew by the stables. And he was certain that one of them was Sir Charles Gerard, the Sheriff.

Folio VI

Tom's prediction of bad weather proved to be accurate; sitting in the boredom of his lesson the following morning, he listened as a fierce gale drove the rain against the windows in sudden gusts, as if unseen hands were throwing gravel at the panes of glass. Ghostly howls of wind echoed down the chimneys and through the corridors of the Hall until it sounded like a house possessed. Tapestries, hung on the walls to keep draughts at bay, swayed drunkenly to and fro. Tom shivered and wrapped his jacket even more tightly around him.

Damn these summer rains! he thought, as he puzzled over the mysteries of Latin verbs. I hope Mary's comfortable. At least the stables are dry. But I wish we'd managed to get some food to her.

He glanced at the schoolroom window and sighed. Outside the rain continued to fall, turning the land into a quagmire. Overhead, the clouds were low and grey, driven on by a ferocious wind that that tore up trees and blew branches down to the ground.

By midday, the storm abated, and a weak watery sun broke through the cloud, bringing a warm freshness. Their studies over, Kate and Tom ran to the stables, trying to avoid the puddles. Small droplets of water sparkled like jewels in the sunshine, and branches of various sizes lay strewn across the paths. The stables could only be reached by stepping from muddy path to muddy path.

Mary was waiting for them in the stables, a little better, but still tired and frail.

"We've brought you some food," said Kate, holding out the bread and cheese. "It's not much but it's better than nothing."

Mary took the food and smiled weakly.

"Thanks." She sank her teeth into the bread and chewed hungrily.

Kate sat down next to her in the straw.

"We were worried about you," she said. "They searched the Hall looking for a traitor—but they didn't find him."

"I know," replied Mary. "They didn't find me neither."

"Why not? They turned the Hall inside out."

Tom wondered just how thorough Sir Charles' men had been.

"Don't know. But they didn't come in here. I stayed hidden though, just in case," Mary mumbled through a mouthful of cheese. "This is good."

Kate was silent for a moment.

"Let's play something." She turned eagerly to Mary. "How about 'Hide and Seek'?"

But Mary shook her head.

"I can't play. I can hardly move. But you play and I'll watch."

Kate thought again, then said, "I know. Let's play 'Executions'. Tom, you can be the King, and I'll be the Queen pleading for my life. Mary can be a woman in the crowd, watching."

Tom grinned wickedly at her, then said, "Even better, you be the Queen and plead for your life... and I'll be the executioner."

Eagerly, Kate jumped up.

"Right," he said, looking severely at Kate. "Start pleading, Queen."

Kate put on her most pitiful expression, her eyes wide and her mouth turned down.

"Please, my Lord. I've done nothing wrong. Please let me live."

Tom and Mary burst out laughing.

"That was really bad, Kate. 'Please my Lord'," he mimicked her words in a high-pitched whining voice.

Kate's down turned mouth trembled and for a moment, Tom thought she was going to cry. Suddenly she exploded into peals of laughter.

"Stop making me laugh, Tom. You always do this. You did it last Sunday in church."

"Well, it's all that Latin. I can't understand a word of it. What really annoys me is how Father's always talking about an *English* church and not following Rome—and we have to listen to Latin for hours on end. If it was in

English it might mean something," Tom grumbled.

"Well, you should pay more attention in your lessons then. At least you get to do interesting things. All I do is sew," replied Kate. "That sampler Mother's making me do is just impossible. And yesterday I spent the whole morning stitching four letters of the alphabet and I had to unpick all of them."

"You're lucky. I've worked in the kitchens since I were eight. And I can't understand what's being said in church either." Mary's voice was low and quiet.

Tom shuffled his feet and looked at her. Not for the first time, he thought about the differences in their lives.

"Well," he said. "At least you're safely out of the way. Mother's hardly going to thrash you for sewing something wrong or cooking the wrong rabbit. Not quite the same as doing badly at Grammar, is it? Or climbing the wrong tree."

Kate looked sideways at her brother and frowned.

"The tree *was* in the churchyard, Tom. And the cat would have come down on its own."

"I still don't think I deserved...what happened. And Father didn't need to know, did he?"

Tom's voice had a harsh edge to it. I owe Carew for that, he thought, remembering how sore he'd felt after his last whipping, how his whole body ached, how he felt so completely worthless and unloved. He fixed his eyes decisively on some indeterminate point in the distance, then turned abruptly to Kate.

"So, Lady Anne Boleyn, your time has come."

Tom picked up a small branch.

"This can be the axe. Now put your head on that bale and I'll be the French executioner. And don't forget afterwards, to roll your eyes and try to speak."

"How can she speak if she's had her head chopped off?" Mary looked at Tom, a puzzled expression on her face.

"That's what Father told me. He said that the executioner held up Queen Anne's head, and for a full minute her eyes moved in her head and it tried to speak. He saw the mouth opening and closing."

The sound of men approaching made all the children sit up with a start. Hurriedly, they hid themselves under some straw mounds—just in time, for the men came into the stables. Lying completely still lest the rustling straw betray their hiding-place, and breathing as quietly as possible, the children listened intently. Tom recognised one of them instantly by his voice; it was Carew. The other man's voice he didn't know, but he was clearly no stranger to Carew. They were talking in low voices, too quiet to hear their conversation fully, but Tom could just make out the occasional word or phrase.

"...ready?" asked the stranger.

"Yes," came the reply, followed by indistinct mumblings.

"Midsummer it is then..." came the stranger's voice again.

Then there was a brief pause before Carew spoke again.

"Is he safe?"

Who was 'he'? wondered Tom. And safe from what? His heart pounded so fiercely, he was certain they would hear it.

The stranger mumbled his reply.

"Good."

Carew again, thought Tom.

"And make sure this time you keep the damn door shut. Those horses escaping nearly gave the game away. Remember, this is justice for the Faith, and Queen..."

The sounds of rustling straw, fading voices and footsteps told the children that the men were leaving and it was safe to come out from their hiding-place. Although it was quite cosy in the straw, it was also itchy, and tickled their noses. And what's more, it smelt of stale horses.

"What was that all about?" asked Kate.

Tom stayed silent. He could feel the unease returning, the fear rising in his throat. What 'game' was Carew talking about? And which Queen? He turned sharply to Mary.

"Do you know the other man?"

"No," replied Mary. "But there have been other people around the stables I've had to hide in the straw a few times. It could be anybody."

She paused and put her head to one side, her forehead creased into a frown.

"You know that piece of cloth you found, caught on a bush?" she asked.

Kate and Tom nodded.

"Well, I found some more of it, over there in the

corner, the night after the horses disappeared. It's like a cloak or tunic of some kind. I used it to keep warm last night."

She rummaged around in the straw and produced a bundle of grubby cloth. Tom took it and held it up. The material unfolded, and he saw that Mary was right. It *did* look like a tunic—although not a very well-made one. The fabric was roughly woven from undyed wool.

"It looks like a priest's robe!" whispered Kate.

"And there's a search on for a monk from Langford, a White Monk, and this material is kind of white," added Tom.

"You're right!" exclaimed Mary. "And I know that food has gone missing from the kitchens. Some chicken legs, fruit, cheese—and I found chicken bones in a corner over there, with the tunic."

Tom spoke, his voice low and trembling.

"What if the escaped monk stole the food and hid in our stables? That might explain the people you saw."

It was Kate's turn to frown. "But Sir Jacob was there, so you said. If he'd seen something suspicious, he'd have raised the alarm, wouldn't he? And how would a priest get the food anyway?" she asked.

A chill crept up Tom's spine as if an unseen hand had just run its fingers along it. What seemed at first to be a simple case of carelessness was turning into something much more dangerous. If someone had left the stables open for the monk, causing the horses to get loose, that same someone might have provided him with food and a hiding-place. And the only people who had a connection with both places were Mary and Carew. But Mary wasn't at the stables on that day... and Carew had beaten her for being there... and was now making sure she was staying away from the stables. And what was going to happen at Midsummer that was so important he needed to have secret meetings in the stables?

Tom was suddenly very afraid—afraid for Mary, afraid for Kate and himself, afraid for his family. If someone was hiding a priest on the Haswell estate, a priest whose intention it was to kill the King, surely they were now all in danger?

"We have to tell someone," he said abruptly. "Give me that tunic. I'll take it to Father and tell him I found it in the stables."

"Not the stables," squealed Kate. "He'll find Mary..."

Tom looked at Mary. Her livid bruises stood out against her pale flesh.

"Then I'll say it was in the bushes. That should be enough."

He picked up the bundle again and tucked it under his arm.

"We'll be back soon with some more food. Stay hidden," he advised Mary.

She nodded, and he and Kate scurried out of the stables, making sure no-one, especially Carew, was around to see them as they did so.

Right, Slugface, thought Tom grimly. This time you won't get the better of me.

Folio VII

"You've never liked Sir Jacob, have you?" asked Kate, as they raced up the gravel path to the Hall. "He's been with us ever since we moved here—almost one of the family. What's so bad about him? Oh, buttons!"

Her linen farthingale caught on a straggly rose bush, and she tugged impatiently at her skirts to free them, sending a cascade of pink petals to the ground. Tom bent down and untangled the lacy hem of the skirt.

"Carew's always trying to get me in trouble, like at breakfast yesterday. 'I'm sure I saw you near the stables'." Tom twisted his face into a gargoyle-like grimace and gestured grandly with his hands, trying to imitate Carew.

"Sir Jacob doesn't do that," said Kate, laughing. "He hunches his shoulders like an old beggar would. And you *were* near the stables."

Tom scowled at his sister, before resuming his complaint at Carew's treatment of him.

"He was creeping about at night…"

"Maybe he didn't want to disturb anyone?"

"...and he was with Sir Charles Gerard down by the stables—which he normally avoids like fermenting horse-dung. What do you think they were talking about, huh? The price of straw?"

"Tom, the horses had got out, Sir Charles is looking for a traitor...that's not so unusual, is it?"

Kate scuttled after her brother, who had started off again towards the Hall. "You just want him to be doing something wrong, don't you?"

Tom opened his mouth to speak, then shut it again quickly. Kate sees things so simply, he thought. Maybe she's right? Maybe I *am* making Carew into something he's not?

"Well, you could be right about the Sheriff. And the prowling about at night. But what about his meeting with Mr. Mystery in the stables, eh? And the tunic we found?"

He felt a warm smugness when Kate had no answer. They climbed the stone steps to the Hall and headed for their father's study. The door was slightly open. Tom knocked softly and waited.

"Come in!"

Sir Richard was at his desk, papers strewn across it. He sighed as he scribbled across one of them. A small pile of gold coins glinted in the light from the leaded window of the room.

"Yes?"

"I've found something in the...er...bushes that I think you should..." began Tom.

His father's stern look interrupted his tentative

opening. Tom shuffled his feet awkwardly.

"What is it? Let me see it, quick. I am extremely busy, as you can see."

Tom held out the grubby bundle and placed it gently on the desk. Sir Richard's face contorted into a grimace of disgust.

"An old cloth? You interrupt me at my accounts to show me these old rags? Get them out of my sight! I have better things to do!"

His voice cracked like a leather horsewhip and his eyes bored into Tom's as he leant over his desk. Tom felt his legs beginning to tremble.

"No, Father. You don't understand. You see, it's a priest's robe…"

"It's a waste of my time, that's what it is! God's Blood! Haven't you something worthwhile to do? Latin? Grammar?"

Tom could see his father was preparing himself for one of his long tirades, and he stiffened his back and waited. There was no way out of this one, surely?

But the expected lecture didn't come. Sir Richard glared once more at Tom, and then said, curtly, "Go, now, and take this louse-infested rag with you. I have important financial matters to address."

Tom picked up the tunic and tiptoed softly to the door. Kate was waiting outside, hopping from foot to foot.

"Well?"

"Well nothing," he snapped at her. "He didn't want to know. Too busy."

"You did tell him it was a priest's tunic?" She placed her hand on his arm and shook him insistently.

"Yes, I did. And he's still too busy."

"So what now?"

Tom leant dejectedly against the wall and sighed.

"Why is it that adults never listen? They're always too busy or not interested, or they think we're up to no good."

He reached out and took two apples from a pewter bowl on a table nearby and was about to pocket them when Master Hollindrake came round the corner.

"Ah, Master Thomas."

The tutor's voice pierced the silence like a Spanish cutthroat's rapier. Tom jumped, wondering if he'd seen him acquire the apples. He slid them deftly into Kate's pockets. No point in risking a beating, he thought, surreptitiously stuffing the tunic behind a tapestry.

"Master Thomas, just the person I was looking for. I have a…er…special errand to perform in the village and, as it's market day, I thought you could accompany me. It will be an exceptionally fine opportunity for you to undertake that sketching activity you were so enthusiastic about earlier."

Tom smiled at his tutor and replied without hesitation.

"I would be most grateful for such an opportunity, sir. Indeed, I shall assemble my scriptorial implements immediately and meet you by the equine accommodation."

Master Hollindrake stared at him for a brief moment, frowned and left in the direction of the stables.

"What *are* you talking about?" asked Kate. "What's eck...whatever you said?"

"Stables," said Tom, and turned to his sister grinning widely. "Why use one word when you can use twenty?"

Kate still looked puzzled. "And why are you so keen to spend an afternoon working with Master H?"

Still grinning, Tom replied, "I won't be with him and I won't be working. His 'special errand' will be with some village girl—and I'll be able to wander round the village."

"But what about me?" Kate squealed. "Can't I come?"

"You don't draw," said Tom. "But you could take those apples to Mary."

He bounded off through the Hall and down the steps. Any opportunity for a ride was worth taking and this promised to be no exception. The sun was already casting its rosy afternoon glow over the landscape, bathing the lush fields and rocky hillsides with a warm radiance.

In the distance, small white dots of sheep grazed contentedly, clinging tenaciously to the steep craggy hills which rose from the valley. Lower down, a deep gash of green revealed the presence of the fast-flowing River Lang, a rich provider of fish for the Haswell kitchens. The hedgerows which bounded the road were in full bloom, the blue of the cornflowers contrasting with the bright red of the poppies, and bees and butterflies danced among the flowers, flitting from one blossom to another.

A short time later, Tom and his tutor were at the

crossroads in the centre of the village, close to the church where every Sunday, without fail, the Haswell family and their servants would attend the service. On such days, the village would be filled with a quiet decorous murmuring as people walked devoutly to perform their worship.

But this day, was very different, and Tom felt a buzz of anticipation, like a small bird wriggling inside him, as they rode through the village to find somewhere to sit and sketch. The open space of the crossroads was a crowded mass of people, animals and carts, all milling around in the muddy street, a hustle of movement, as each tried to find a path through to the edge of the street. The air was filled with the shouts of people selling fruit, ironware, cheap roughly shaped pottery, squares of woollen cloth. A wooden trestle stood in one corner loaded with small rounds of wheat and rye bread. The smell of roasting poultry drifted around them like a warm cloak, and as they rode further on, Tom caught sight of a man turning a spit with whole chickens on it, the hot fat dripping from the plump flesh onto the glowing logs below.

"Now Master Thomas, I have to leave you now for my special errand. It may take me some time. Have you identified anything which inspires your artistic talents?"

Tom scanned the market place quickly, hoping to see something that was both interesting and easy to sketch. One of the windowless houses with its walls of baked mud—that would be easy enough. Or one of the small speckled birds that hopped around pecking animatedly at wisps of pale yellow straw. Maybe one of the fat black and white pigs that snuffled around between the trestles would stay still long enough for him to make a decent sketch.

Then suddenly, his eye registered something known to him, something that made his heart beat instantly faster. At the side of the crossroads, almost hidden by the chicken man, was a woman selling summer fruits and wild flowers. Her face was tired and drawn, but clean, which was in striking contrast with the faces of the other villagers, whose skin looked ingrained with dirt. Her clothes too had seen better days.

But it was not the woman's pale face, nor her old clothes which made Tom stop and stare: it was the fair-haired boy beside her, selling bundles of sticks, whose face struck a chord of memory within him. He, too, was pale and shabbily dressed, and although one or two people had exchanged a groat or two for his bundles of firewood, it was clear that a sunny day in June wasn't going to be particularly profitable.

"Master Hollindrake," began Tom. "I think I'd like to walk around to find a good subject to sketch. Would that be acceptable, sir?" Tom kept his gaze firmly on the boy, afraid that he would disappear once he looked away.

"I think that would be an excellent idea, Master Thomas," replied the tutor. "But choose somewhere away from the crowds. I will meet you here shortly, with your work, when the church clock strikes four times. "

Tom dismounted briskly and tethered his horse a little way from the square. Surely it couldn't be! He must be mistaken, his eyes playing tricks on him. His keen eyes

53

eagerly sought out the boy he'd seen earlier. Where was he? Where had he gone? Then he heard a plaintive cry.

"Firewood, a groat a bundle!" it called. "Firewood!"

Now moving almost at a run, Tom squeezed through crowd of people, darting sideways on one occasion to avoid a pig that got loose. With mouth dry and heart racing faster than a hungry lurcher on a rabbit hunt, he followed the sound of the voice until he found himself directly in front of the boy. One glance at the pale upturned face told Tom he was not mistaken. The face, although now much thinner and sadder than he remembered it, was unmistakeably the face of his friend, Edward Fishwyck!

"Edward!" gasped Tom. He stared at the boy's grimy homespun jacket and ill-fitting breeches. Small ragged threads poked out from small moth-holes in his woollen cap, beneath which poked wisps of straggly brown hair. "What are you doing here? What's happened to you?"

Edward looked down at the bundles of sticks at the side of his battered, misshapen boots. There was a harsh edge to his voice when he spoke.

"Selling firewood. What does it look like?"

Tom opened his mouth to speak, but no words would come. There was so much to say, so much he wanted to say. Edward got to his feet stiffly, and straightened his back. He looked Tom straight in the eyes, his chin jutting forward.

"Surprised, Tom? You shouldn't be. You'll have heard the rumours by now."

Tom forced himself to speak, at once glad and saddened by his old friend's appearance.

"I heard some talk, servants' gossip mainly, about your father…" The lie stuck in his throat and his voice tailed off as he struggled to find the right words.

Edward helped him out of his dilemma. "You should always listen to servants' gossip, Tom. You'd be amazed at what they know. Did they say my father was dead?"

Tom shook his head. An ache grew deep in his chest and he felt his throat tightening as if an unseen hand had clamped itself around his neck. He turned his eyes away from Edward's penetrating stare. For the first time he noticed the lengthening shadows of the nearby buildings.

"He died a traitor's death, Tom. Do you know what that means?" Edward spat the words out. He paused and waited for Tom's response. When none came, he continued. "My father, Tom. My dear, laughing, loving father—murdered in public like a common thief. He was hanged, disembowelled, beheaded, and his body cut into quarters."

Edward spoke the words heavily and clearly. Each one struck Tom's heart like a blunt dagger. How much more of this horror was there to endure? But Edward hadn't finished. It was almost as if he wanted to hurt him, to make him share his pain. "What was left of him was displayed to the public in various parts of London, to serve as a warning to them."

Edward's eyes moistened, but no tears fell.

"Are you sure?" whispered Tom, his stomach

churning with horror. "I mean, maybe he escaped? You must have some hope of that."

Edward shook his head. "They made us watch. I was so close I could have reached out and touched his blood, still warm on the executioner's sword. He's dead. I have no doubt of that, and no hope. "

Tom swallowed hard. His dry lips stuck together.

"I'm sorry, truly sorry. He was a good man, and I will always remember him. I wish..." What? To take Edward home with him? To live at Myersford? Impossible.

"I'm supposed to be sketching now, but..." He hesitated again. Edward was his best friend and his disappearance left an empty space in his life. Much as he loved his sister, it just wasn't the same. Kate played different games and talked about dresses and dolls. The dull chiming of the church bell penetrated his thoughts.

"Can we meet somewhere?" he blurted out suddenly. "Do you live nearby?"

Edward stared at him curiously, and for a moment Tom thought he was going to say no. But he appeared to reconsider.

"I'll meet you after church on Sunday. By the bridge over the stream."

Tom nodded. Then out of the corner of his eye, he saw Master Hollindrake looking for him.

"I have to go," he whispered, hurriedly. "Till Sunday. I'll be there—promise."

He spun on his heels, pushed his way through the crowd of people and headed towards the churchyard. He cast one last look across the throng of people to see if Edward was still there, but the crowd was too bustling and too dense; he couldn't see him.

The journey home passed in a blur; even Master Hollindrake's annoyance at his lack of sketching failed to make any impact on Tom. He burned with fury at Edward's plight, and his father's horrific death, but to see his friend again, his best friend, was worth any punishment. All he could think about was meeting Edward again. And he had no doubts that he would meet him again—despite his father's instruction that such an encounter was forbidden. The only doubt in his mind was whether he should tell Kate or not. Could he trust her? She wouldn't tell anyone deliberately; but would she reveal it in a careless moment?

As he dismounted, Tom decided that he would tell her. After all, she had a new friend in Mary, so why shouldn't he have one too?

Middlemore the groom led the horses away, and Tom sped off to find her. She was waiting for him, watching out of a window, and he smiled cheerfully as she ran to meet him. But his smile faded the moment he saw her pale face, with its anxious darting eyes. Something had happened in his absence.

"What is it?" he whispered, all thoughts of Edward vanishing in a swirl of panic.

"It's Mary." Her words fell like stones in a deep, motionless pond. "She's gone!"

Folio VIII

"Gone?"

Tom stared silently as his sister's eyes welled up with tears. A rapid drumbeat pounded in his chest. Gone where? He breathed on slowly, then out again, trying to control the swelling panic within him.

"I went to the stables with the apples for her, and a blanket, but she wasn't there. It was empty."

Slowly, two large tears spilled over Kate's pallid cheeks and disappeared into her lace collar.

"Maybe she went out for a walk, or was hiding somewhere? I'm sure there's a good reason for this."

Tom's voice was calm and soothing, and betrayed nothing of his rising fears. What if Carew or his friend had come back and found her? Crept up on her while she was sleeping?

"Can we go to the stables and look, Tom? Please? Will you come with me, now?"

One glance at his sister's wide beseeching eyes was enough. Tom grabbed her hand and pulled her, running, off down the path to the stables. The vivid colours of the summer flowers flashed by in a fragrant rush as they sped by, until they finally skidded to a halt in front of the stables in a flurry of gravel.

"Sh!" he warned Kate. There was no knowing who or what lay in wait for them.

Tentatively, he stepped forward, as if each movement would disturb some angry monster. But the stables were deserted save for the Haswell horses—no monster—and no Mary. Just the occasional shuffle of a restless horse or an impatient snort. Tom picked up a pitchfork and threaded the prongs gently through the pale yellow straw. Nothing.

At the sound of rustling straw behind him, he turned sharply. The muscles in his neck and shoulders contracted into a tight knot of pain.

"What are you doing here?" said a gruff voice behind them.

Tom whirled round startled, and found himself face to face with John Middlemore, the chief groom.

"You looking for something?" he enquired abruptly.

"Er...no. At least...I'm not sure...I..."

Tom hesitated and eyed the groom warily. Did he know about Mary? Surely a man who spent all his time down by the stables would have noticed something. And how well did he know Carew?

" 'Cause, Master Tom, if you think you can hang around here all day with Mistress Kate, you can think again. I've got work to do—special work for Sir Jacob."

Tom's heart missed a beat and he winced as Kate clutched at his arm. Special work for Carew? Now what could that be?

He glanced sideways at Kate and pressed his lips together as if warning her not to say anything. The walls of the stables seemed to close in on him.

"We could help you, if you like," he offered, struggling to keep his voice calm and even.

Kate frowned at him, but said nothing.

"Could you indeed?"

John Middlemore raised an enquiring eyebrow and folded his arms defensively.

"And just why do you want to do that, hmm?"

Tom shuffled his feet awkwardly as the groom stared at him intently. It was as if his grey eyes could pierce into your very soul, thought Tom. What was the man thinking behind that bright, steely gaze?

"Sir Jacob was most particular," continued Middlemore. "Told me exactly what to do and where."

His eyes narrowed and he looked curiously at Tom. The groom's imposing frame, broad-shouldered and muscular, towered above him, and for a fleeting moment, Tom wondered if he should run quickly.

"Maybe he sent you here to make sure I did a proper job? To spy on me?"

"No...no," stammered Tom. "We were looking for... a... fox. Yes, we thought we saw a fox round here, and we could help... someone... catch it."

He breathed out long and hard, the knots of anxiety

untangling as he did so. Beside him, Kate relaxed her grip on him.

"A fox?"

The groom continued to eye him warily.

"I've seen no fox around here. Look, I've got to clear all this straw. Sir Jacob needs somewhere to store some new farming tools. If you want to help, there are some pitchforks over there."

He gestured towards a dark corner of the stable where some old rusty tools were propped up against the wall. Tom went to get two of them and started to move the straw into a neat pile in one of the stalls.

"Why did you ask if Carew—Sir Jacob—had sent us to spy on you?" Tom asked abruptly.

Middlemore paused in his straw-shifting and rested his pitchfork against the wall. He hesitated a moment before replying.

"Sir Jacob seems to take much upon himself these days. Since when have the stables been his concern? Always hanging around, he is, wanting to know where I'm working. There's nothing wrong with my work. I answer to God and your father, and no other."

There was a harsh edge to Middlemore's voice, and Tom wondered if this was a good time to ask him about Mary. It sounded as if he had no time for Carew—but if he had found Mary, surely he would have said something? Perhaps it's better to keep quiet, he decided.

But a deep ache of concern for Mary still lingered. What had happened to her?

In the distance, the church clock chimed five times.

"We have to go—they'll miss us at the Hall," said Tom.

The groom nodded and touched his cap, but his eyes still retained a glint of suspicion. Abruptly, he leaned forward to pick up his pitchfork again. As he did so, Tom saw a bright flash from his neck. Something glinted there, something gold and gleaming, a chain, was it? Middlemore reached for it and hastily pulled the neck of his shirt together.

That's strange, thought Tom. That looked like jewellery of some sort, expensive jewellery. How could a groom afford something like that? And why wear it when you spend your days in the stables anyway?

Still puzzled, Tom hurried off in the direction of the Hall, with Kate at his heels. The clouds had a reddish cast to them, and long yellow Jacob's Ladders streaked down from behind them like golden ribbons.

"So where is she?" asked Kate, her tone insistent and quavering.

"I don't know," replied Tom. "But if any harm has come to her, we'll find out soon enough. You know how people gossip in the village. Maybe she felt better and went back to her family?"

"Maybe," said Kate. "But she could have left a note or something."

Tom said nothing. Once more, his fears for Mary began to swamp him. If Carew has found her, and beaten her again…she was weak from the first beating. Would she have survived a second? He glanced up at the sky and tried to put his worries aside.

In the silence, his stomach gurgled loudly and Kate prodded his belly firmly.

"It's nearly suppertime, Tom. Tell your tummy to be patient—it's always making noises."

"That's because I'm always hungry," he replied.

"What have you done today to make you so hungry, then? Kate's tone became sullen and whining, and Tom wondered if she'd had as much excitement as he had. He cleared his throat.

"If I tell you something, do you promise not to tell?"

Kate looked up at him, her eyes suddenly eager.

"Something that happened today, in the village?"

"Yes."

"Is it something bad?"

Tom thought for a moment. Was it bad? He wasn't sure. It was good to see Edward again, to talk and laugh with him. But their lives had changed so much. And Edward's father's fate?

"Sort of, but good as well."

No sound disturbed the silence that surrounded them, not even a bird-call.

"Yes, I promise," answered Kate.

Tom breathed in deeply.

"I met Edward today at the market. Master Hollindrake went off on his 'errand' and I was looking for something to sketch. And then I saw Edward selling firewood."

Kate gasped and put her hand to her mouth.

"But, Tom. Father expressly forbade you to..."

"I know," he snapped. "But I couldn't help it. We were friends and he's poor...oh, Kate. His father's dead....and I couldn't walk past and pretend he wasn't there..."

Hot tears, for so long held tightly within him, sprang to his eyes, and burned like sand-grains on his eyelids. Tom swallowed hard, trying to force them back. He turned away and roughly wiped his sleeve over his face.

"Tom, what is it?"

"You don't want to know. Just that his father's dead, in a horrible way, and I feel so...guilty."

Yes, guilty, he thought. As if it were my fault. As if my father and his fine friends in their big houses had caused all Edward's troubles. Surely they could have done something, spoken up for them? They were friends after all, weren't they?

"Don't be silly, Tom. You've done nothing wrong." Kate paused and a flicker of alarm crossed her face. "You're not going to see him again, are you?"

Tom stayed silent.

"Oh, Tom."

"Sunday, after church. Are you coming with me? We could ask him about Mary."

Kate hesitated, and then nodded.

"But only this once."

"In that case," replied Tom, "I've got something else to tell you. I found a secret passageway, and if we're quick, I can show you before supper."

Kate looked at him askance and smiled.

"A secret passageway? Where? Where does it lead?"

"From the pantry corridor to Father's study."

Tom smiled. A delicious thought entered his head. A crafty, devious thought that sneaked in like a fox on a moonlit night.

"We could spy on Carew."

"You're not serious!" Kate's blue eyes stared up at him.

"Can you think of a better way of finding out what he's up to? Come on."

He turned and ran down the path to the servants' entrance. Several bedraggled hens were pecking aimlessly at the ground. They clucked anxiously and flapped away as Tom and Kate made for the doorway.

"Careful!" cautioned Tom. "There's someone around. Wait a minute."

Pressed closely into the shadows of the corridor, Tom watched as a maidservant carried bread and fruit out of the pantry. When he was sure that she wouldn't return, he motioned to Kate to follow him and led the way to the false panel. Once inside the narrow passageway, surrounded by the stifling gloom, Tom inched along. Kate clung on tightly to him.

"Careful here," he whispered. "There are some boxes."

"Boxes of what?" whispered back Kate.

"Don't know, but don't walk into them."

He edged cautiously around them, stopping once to

untangle Kate's full skirt from one of them. He was about to move on, deeper into the passage, when he hesitated.

"Wait a minute, Kate. Let's see if we can work one of these lids open."

He knelt down by the nearest pile of boxes and slid his finger along the rough edge of one of the lids, looking for a loose section he could work free.

But no. The lid was nailed down firmly. He tried another box, and another. But again he had no luck. Whoever had nailed the lids down, intended them to stay that way.

Tom gestured to Kate to follow him once more and he guided her along the passageway.

Soon they reached the blank wall and Tom whispered, "This is the study."

He was about to open the panel to show Kate, when his attention was caught by the sound of muffled voices. Someone was in the study! Gently, he placed his finger on Kate's lips to silence her, and felt her nod in understanding. He listened, his ear close to the wall panel.

"Is that all? There should be more than that."

His father's voice, tight and anxious. A mumbled response, indistinct. Tom moved closer to the wall panel.

"We replaced all the hay we lost in the fire, didn't we? So we must have more than this."

"My lord, we did."

Carew! And being his usual grovelling self. Tom could almost see him, hunched and fawning, like some pathetic lapdog.

"We replaced it all, ready for the winter, and paid a goodly price for it, too. But it appears we will need more, Sir Richard, and that will cost..." Again, a mumble.

So Carew got it wrong, did he? A pulse of excitement throbbed in Tom's chest. This was excellent news!

"And the money from the seven foals we sold? Where's that in these devilish accounts of yours, eh?"

"If you look here, my lord, in this inventory here..."

A sudden thud and a rustle of falling papers told Tom that his father had tired of Carew and his books.

"And you still need more money? I can't believe it!"

Behind the panel, Tom felt a prickle of fear on his scalp. For a fleeting moment, he almost felt sorry for Carew. But then he remembered the beating he'd given Mary.

"So we need more money, and more hay? Damn it, Carew! I pay you to manage my accounts. I expect to be in profit. And we still have a Midsummer Feast to pay for! You know how Lady Elizabeth entertains—expensively!"

Tom shifted his position slowly and deliberately, his ear still pressed tightly against the panel. Beside him Kate's regular, controlled breathing told him she was listening too.

"My lord, the foals brought us in less money than expected, and we have to pay the servants soon. St John's Day is coming and..."

"Excuses! Feeble excuses! You have failed me, Carew. Maybe...maybe I could save some money by sacking some less valuable servants, hmm? Maybe I could start with you?"

67

The sudden vibration of the door slamming reached Tom's ear and he pulled back from the panel with a start. A tremor of excitement ran through him. Carew sacked? Kicked out and sent packing? With no job and no money? That would serve him right. Tom stiffened his jaw and smiled a wide smug smile.

"Come on," he hissed to Kate. "It must be suppertime. We'd best not be late."

The children turned and threaded their way through the gloomy passageway to the exit panel.

"What was Father talking about, Tom? He was really angry."

Kate's whispers floated over her shoulder and echoed in the darkness.

"I think Carew's in trouble." No point in telling her there was a problem with money. She wouldn't understand.

"Father said he would sack him. And then he'd have no money to buy his fancy, expensive clothes, would he?" Kate peered up at Tom, her question hanging in the silence.

Tom stopped abruptly. Of course! Why hadn't *he* seen it? His father wasn't the most generous employer in Lancashire, so people said—far from it. And Carew had very expensive tastes—clothes, books—which an accountant's salary couldn't possibly satisfy. And what about Carew's sudden liking for the stables? Hadn't John Middlemore said Carew was always checking up on him?

A surge of anger pulsated through Tom's body. After

all Carew had said at breakfast about burglars and now it seemed the man could be nothing but a thief, a fraudster! A leech who used other people for his own devious ends. He had to be stopped. But how?

Folio IX

"But why do I have to go? I hate going to church. It's dull, it's cold—and worst of all, it's in Latin."

Tom picked up his velvet breeches and short velvet cloak and glared at them, his lips clamped together in a tight hard line.

Lady Elizabeth sighed and raised her eyes upwards, as if seeking divine assistance.

"You have to go, Tom. You know that. It's a small price to pay for eternal life. And it pleases your father. Now get dressed quickly. Your neck-ruff is ready and starched."

She turned her attention to Kate and adjusted the stiff farthingale under her gown. Kate looked over her mother's head at Tom and raised her eyebrows quizzically.

"I thought you wanted to go?" she mouthed.

Tom frowned back at her, warning her. Of course he wanted to go. He had so much to tell Edward, so many months of friendship to regain. But a sudden enthusiasm for worship in a wooden pew so hard it turned his entire body to stone would certainly make his parents suspicious. Much better to pretend, he decided. That way there are no awkward questions.

He continued to feign reluctance all the way to church, his outward gloom matching the weather. A low white blanket of cloud hung over Myersford, threatening the village and surrounding fields with summer showers. There was a strange echoing stillness as they walked up the path to the parish church, as if another storm were brewing in the west. As he followed his father, Tom's thoughts were of nothing but Edward and their promised meeting. 'Where was he living now?' he wondered. If it was nearby…

"Good morning, Sir Richard."

Harry Wiswall, the constable, was waiting to greet the day's worshippers. Tom smiled politely at him as he passed into the church. No doubt anyone not attending would be reminded of their duties.

A low murmuring incantation resounded through the darkness of the stone church, now devoid of its statues and candles, following the king's order to remove them. Tom took his place in the Haswell pew at the side of the church, the family crest newly carved into the dark wood of the pew-end.

Despite Master Hollindrake's meticulous attention to the study of Latin, Tom stumbled through the responses. *Pater Noster* was the limit of his comprehension. Above him, a row of carved angels stared down at him, disapprovingly.

This is dragging by much more slowly than usual, he thought. He ached with hunger and fidgeted. His mother glared sternly at him. Shifting his position on the pew, he sighed loudly; it wasn't his fault he wasn't allowed breakfast before the service. As the congregation rose to incant the 'Te Deum', Tom sighed. Tedium, more like.

The best thing about sitting here, thought Tom, during one particularly lengthy prayer, is that you can look around and see who else is bored. He remembered the secret signals that he and Edward had worked out together, so they could communicate in the silence of the Mass. Where was he now? In his own church? Or already by the stream, waiting? A sharp ripple of anticipation ran through him as he thought once more of their secret meeting. Inwardly, he smiled. Carew couldn't stop them. Sunday was his day for visiting his family in Langford.

Half-opening one eye, Tom lifted his head slightly, and studied the congregation. John Middlemore was there, head lowered devoutly in prayer. Harry Wiswall stood, head bowed, by the door, ready to deal with anyone who wasn't worshipping wholeheartedly. There was the rest of the Wiswall family, dutifully kneeling, as were the rest of the congregation. And there, sitting next to Mistress Wiswall, was the slight but familiar figure of Mary! Even from this distance, Tom could see the yellow bruises on her arms, fading remnants of Carew's beating. So she was safe! But how ...?

Tom sighed inwardly, relief invading his body like a warm infusion of herbs. To know she was safe was good news. Maybe he and Kate could speak to her at the end of Mass? Ask her how she came to leave the stables?

Then Tom saw something which made him suddenly open both eyes. At the rear of the church, in the pews known as Strangers' Gallery, was one of the men that Tom had seen talking with Carew outside the stables the day after the horses went missing.

He was well-dressed in richly coloured clothes, an elegant ruff and full breeches. So, not a villager, thought Tom. A gentleman, by the look of him. What's he doing in Myersford? And what business has he got with Carew?

Tom pulled his cloak around him and shuffled on the wooden pew, trying to relieve some of the numbness.

Then his attention was held by a curious thing. The ever vigilant Harry Wiswall, although his head was held as if in prayer, was clearly watching the man; Tom could see his eyes blinking. His heart started to beat faster. A stranger who attracted the constable's attention, a stranger who was also a friend of Carew's—and who was soon to be entertained at Myersford Hall—what was going on?

The prayers ended and the congregation raised their heads and turned attentively towards the high altar. Tom tried to avoid looking directly at the man, turning his attention instead to the priest, who was about to speak. After the priest had uttered the Dominus Vobiscum, the service was over. Tom strode towards the door as briskly as decency would allow, but his mother called him back.

"Tom! Your hat. You've left it behind."

Tom pushed his way back and snatched up his hat

from the pew. Now the whole world and his wife would be blocking his way out! At this rate, he'd never get to the stream. What if Edward had gone? And Mary? He had to find out how she came to be with the Wiswalls.

The stranger also made to depart, hat in hand and headed for the door, bowing politely to Sir Richard and Lady Haswell as he did so. So his father knew him too?

Once outside, Tom breathed in deeply to fill his lungs with fresh air. His eyes alert and shining, he looked round for Mary. Where was she? He was sure he'd seen her leaving the church just in front of him.

He glanced down the path to the arched lych-gate just in time to see her heading in the direction of the smithy along with the rest of the Wiswalls.

I've no chance of catching up with her now, thought Tom. But it's good to know she's not…

He couldn't bring himself to recall the terrible visions of her fate that had haunted him since that day when they found the stables empty. But his relief was tinged with annoyance. She could have waited for them, could have explained what had happened to her. If not to ease his mind, then at least for Kate's sake.

He turned back to rejoin his father, who was by now in deep conversation with Hargreaves, their nearest neighbour. Now to find Edward. He had his excuse ready.

"Please, sir," he asked his father. "May Kate and I go to watch the fish in the stream?"

"Of course," replied his father. "But be sensible and don't be long."

Tom and Kate sped off in the direction of the stream. They scrambled down the gentle banking and found Edward sitting on a large stone under the bridge, idly throwing stones into the stream. He raised his head and smiled as he saw them scrambling down the bank. By his side was a sack which contained sticks.

"The storm made my job easy," grinned Edward. "Plenty of branches lying around. By winter they'll be ready for burning."

"That's how you live—selling firewood?" panted Tom.

"Partly. My mother sells flowers and fruit—and she's an excellent dressmaker, so we don't do too badly. We moved across the valley to Langford. It's different now—the really good news is—no more lessons, especially Latin!"

"As good as that?"

Despite the obvious benefit of no Latin, Tom felt a deep ache of sadness inside, and his throat tightened sharply once more as Edward unknowingly reminded him of their differing fortunes.

"How are things with you?" continued Edward.

Tom sat down next to him, and Kate prodded the water with a fallen branch in a vain attempt to build a small dam.

"Where do I start?" he began. "Things have been so odd lately. We had a barn fire, then some horses got loose, and now Carew…"

Tom paused. How could he voice his real worries, that

Carew was involved in something much more serious than mismanaging his father's estate? What evidence did he have for that unspoken fear lurking in the depths of his mind?

"Who's Carew?"

Edward made no attempt to hide his curiosity.

"My father's accountant, Sir Jacob Carew. He manages the estates and finances. Really thinks he's important, but he's a slimy, two-faced sneak. You might know him. He comes from Langford."

Edward pulled down the corners of his mouth and thought hard.

"No, I don't think I know any Carews in Langford. So what's he up to?"

"Well, he spends a lot of time at the stables even though horses make him ill, supposedly. And he blamed one of the kitchenmaids for letting the horses loose, but it wasn't her—and he knows it. He sneaks around at night and I tried to tell my father but he's always too busy. And the groom, Middlemore…"

"John Middlemore?"

Edward's eyes narrowed.

Tom nodded. "You know him?"

"Yes, very well. He's a good man, local. Knows all about horses. In fact, he used to work for my father before…"

Edward's eyes misted over with a shiny gloss. Then he cleared his throat hurriedly.

"He's had some sadness in his life too, so I've heard.

His brother was…died a few months ago."

"I didn't know that. Was it the sleeping sickness?"

This was really something to worry about. If the sleeping sickness returned, who knows how many would die? It had taken half the village last time.

"No, it was sudden, but he wasn't ill. But what about Carew?"

Tom resumed his tale, surprised by the abrupt change of subject. It was almost as if Edward was hiding something.

"Well, John Middlemore says he's always asking him where he's working, checking up on him. And really it's none of his business. He even thought we were spying on him for Carew. And then something really frightening happened."

Edward listened intently as Tom quickly told him of the search of the house and the missing priest.

"And what's really worrying," went on Tom, "is that we found a priest's robe…" He stopped short, remembering what his father had said about the Fishwycks being loyal to Rome. Could he trust Edward? What if he already knew about the plot?

Edward stayed silent for a moment and scrutinised the trickling stream carefully. His brow furrowed a little and he inhaled deeply before he spoke.

"Going to church is supposed to be for our good, but it's brought nothing but unhappiness to my family. My father was a good man; he was honest, hard-working, he managed the estate well. He would never have harmed a hair of the King's beard—and yet they said he was a traitor. And it was all to do with religion."

He glanced away momentarily. No sound was heard save the gentle rush of the stream as it made its way towards the River Lang.

"I'm sure there is a priest on the run. In fact, I think there are probably quite a lot—the King's planning to close all the monasteries and take their land and money. You've seen the Priory at Langford, haven't you? When the King's commissioners came, they smashed all the statues, and ordered the priests to leave and find other work. That's happening all over the country, Tom. And if your family are even suspected of harbouring this priest— well, that's treason."

Edward's face was flushed, his lips pale. He paused. His eyes glistened suddenly as if someone had blown dust into them. A harsh note came into his voice. "How do you think you got your house, Tom? Do you think your father bought it?"

Tom's lower jaw dropped open. Who did Edward think he was? Friends didn't speak to friends in such a fashion. This was supposed to be a reunion, two old friends meeting after many long months apart.

"Edward, I..."

But Edward didn't hear him. His eyes focused on some unseen object in the sky.

"I remember the day they came to search our house. It was the day they took my father away. His hands were bound behind his back. They threw him down the steps of the Manor. The last thing he said to me was, 'Don't worry. I'll come back to you. Take care of your mother.' The next time I saw him was the day they executed him."

A solid lump of pain swelled within Tom and his head pounded to an invisible rhythm. The leaves on the alders overhanging the stream rattled as a gusty wind caught them. Edward turned to Tom.

"Your house was owned by the Stanley family. Of the Old Religion, like me, and they resisted the King's new church—like my father did. They lost their lands, their house and their title. So remember, Tom—it's a traitor's house you live in. Be very careful. I wouldn't wish my family's fate on my worst enemy. No money, no food, no father. You don't know how lucky you are."

Voices overhead intruded on their whispered conversation.

"You'd better go," said Edward. "Watch Carew very carefully. It does sound as if he's involved in something that could bring trouble to your house. But we need real proof. Meet me at the Midsummer Fair in the village— that's if you want to be friends with a poor firewood collector!"

Tom opened his mouth to protest that of course he wanted to be friends with him, but Edward was already halfway across the banking. Tom scurried after him, hoping for one last word, but by the time he reached the top, Edward was nowhere in sight.

"T—o – m."

Kate's three-toned whine made him turn round. She

was at the bottom of the banking, one hand outstretched, the other clinging on to a young sapling.

"I'm stuck."

"Oh, come on." He held out his hand and hauled her up.

They darted off towards the church. Dawdling worshippers still milled around the graveyard and Tom noted with some relief that his father was deep in conversation with the constable. A few of the congregation meandered between the gravestones, occasionally stopping to read the carved inscriptions.

Then, in the farthest corner of the graveyard, where the paupers were buried, Tom saw John Middlemore, head bowed, standing in front of a small mound. In his hands he held a small bunch of wild flowers. No stone marked the mound, which could only have been a grave. The groom bent down and laid the flowers gently on the mound.

Interesting, thought Tom. Edward said he'd lost his brother. I wonder if that's his grave? Sad that he has no headstone though.

He looked around the monuments nearby. Many of them were small, with simple lettering—just a name and a date, and sometimes partially covered with lichen. Others had flowers laid in front of them. But one memorial stood out from all the rest, towered above them, its huge imposing structure casting a shadow over its smaller neighbours.

Head cocked to one side, Tom read the lengthy

inscription. The lettering was ornate, and in places difficult to read, but the name made Tom's heart beat a little faster.

"Here lyeth ye bodie of Lady Margaret STANLEY of Myersforde..."

"I wonder if she was one of the Stanleys who lived in our house?" Tom wondered out loud. He bent down for a closer look.

"...who dyed ye IVth day of December 1514, and of her son Henry STANLEY who dyed ye Vth day of December 1514."

So mother and son died one day apart. Maybe she died giving life to her son, and then he died the next day? It was a common enough story, especially in winter. He sighed. How lucky he and Kate were to have two parents still living.

Then Tom's attention was held by some smaller lettering, in a different script, underneath the main inscription.

"Also her father, Sir William GLOVER of Langford, who departed this life ye XVIIth day of November 1516."

What a fascinating story! She must have been Margaret Glover of Langford, whoever she was, and married Somebody Stanley, and died in childbirth. Perhaps Edward knew them? Maybe some of them still live in Langford?

"She was a fine lady."

A voice behind him cut across his thoughts. Tom turned and saw John Middlemore. The groom's grey eyes stared shrewdly back at him, like a wily hound on a boar hunt.

"Really?"

"Oh, yes. Beautiful. And kind. Always had a smile for you. Married into the Stanleys of Lower Myersford."

Middlemore paused and gazed up at the grand monument. Tom did the same, his eyes tracing the elegant lines of the structure. Lichen had spread over parts of the stonework, giving it a patchwork appearance, and spiders' webs, still glistening with dew, clung tenaciously around the base.

"When she and the child died, it finished her father. They say he died of a broken heart at the loss of his daughter and grandson. But others say it was her brother that did for him."

Tom's eyes narrowed and he peered up at the groom.

"What did he do?"

Middlemore sniffed sharply, and ran his brown leather boots over the uneven grass. A frown appeared across his brow.

"I don't rightly know. I never met him. He moved away from Lancashire. But they say he was wayward and shiftless. Always kept bad company. His father had to pay a fortune to keep him out of jail—so they say."

"And her husband, Lord Stanley?" Tom hardly dared to ask.

"Sir John? He was different after she died. Refused to follow King Henry's religion and paid the usual price for being a recusant. Lost his house and lands, and was taken away for execution at Lancaster."

Tom shuffled his feet, as if his boots were troubling him. So Myersford was once home of these Stanleys? Both Edward and John must have known the family and yet neither seemed to have a grudge against his own family for living there. And despite his father saying the Fishwycks were fools, he was happy to employ their groom, who seemed to have more knowledge of the deeds of Papists than most people. Tom stared up at the man beside him. His tanned face looked as if it had been carved from stone.

A sudden thought flashed into Tom's mind. What if Middlemore was a Papist too? And could he be involved in Carew's strange activities? He complained about Carew, that was true. But that could be just a trick, to cover up...whatever they were involved in. And he certainly wasn't like the other servants. That gold chain, for instance? Where had he got that from? No sign of it today.

And those boots? Tom stared down at the groom's feet. The polished brown leather shimmered with diamonds of summer dew which sparkled in the bright morning light. Those were no servant's boots. So how had Middlemore come by them?

The world of adults, which seemed once to offer security, was now threatening; what other secrets, what strange loyalties, lurked in Myersford? And what hidden dangers?

Folio X

Over the next two days, Tom and Kate kept a watch on Carew—at least, as much of a watch as they could without arousing suspicion. Kate positioned herself in a window-seat to work on her sampler while her mother fussed over the preparations for the Midsummer feast. Over the top of her hooped embroidery, she had an excellent view of the stable yard. Tom, meanwhile, moved his seat to the opposite side of the schoolroom, a manoeuvre which did not escape Master Hollindrake's keen observation.

"And why the change of seat, Master Thomas? Has some young serving wench caught your eye, eh?"

Trust him to think that, thought Tom. Just the sort of thing he *would* think.

He recalled the previous Sunday how, when he returned from his meeting with Edward, Master Hollindrake was absorbed in a cosy conversation with Harry Wiswall's youngest daughter, Jane, who'd worked alongside Mary in the kitchens at Lower Myersford Hall.

"I thought this might be a good place to sketch from,

Master Hollindrake," said Tom, his eyes wide and innocent. There seemed to be no need to mention that from his new position he could see the gardens to the rear of the house, and the southern corner of the orchard.

St John's Day was fast approaching, and the servants were expecting to be paid. Not one of them passed up an opportunity to do some errand for Sir Richard or Lady Haswell, hoping for that extra sixpence for their trouble. With wages at a shilling a day, a generous tip could make a big difference to a labourer's income and put much needed food on the table. So Lower Myersford Hall became a bustling whirlwind of activity; the Great Hall was decked with richly embroidered fabrics and tapestries, deliveries of food arrived daily as Lady Haswell changed her menu yet again. Guests for the Midsummer feast were already arriving with their servants, and all had to be allocated bed-chambers, and provided with food and drink.

Not that it looked much like Midsummer outside. Tom peered gloomily at the window-pane, now streaked with little rivulets of rain. A white blanket of cloud loomed overhead and a fine but persistent drizzle surrounded the landscape like a grey cocoon.

'This is in for the day,' he muttered gloomily. 'If we go outside today, we'll need to find shelter.'

Through the greyness, Tom watched as a constant stream of carters drove heavy loads of cloth, food and decorations past the rear of the hall, to be greeted by eager boys waiting to unload the carts. The warm musty smell of ale permeated the house, which meant that the brewing of the ale for the feast was well underway.

That afternoon, Kate was full of news about the preparations. "We're going to have gingerbread, Tom, and little batter puddings from Yorkshire, and something called French Toast—slices of bread soaked in beaten egg and then cooked. It sounds wonderful. And you should see my new dress! It's *so* grown up—it has white linen sleeves with fine black embroidery on them. Apparently, it's very fashionable in Spain."

Tom listened impatiently to her excited chatter. More than anything he wanted to find out what Carew was doing. Nothing seemed to make any sense at all. Who were the visitors, these friends of Carew's? Where was the priest? And what was going to happen at Midsummer? If only he could find something that would really convince his father that Carew was not to be trusted.

And Middlemore—what was his part in all this? He was hard-working and respectful, no-one could deny that. But there was something un-servant-like about him. The way he spoke, for example, and those fine leather boots. And hadn't a gold chain gone missing from the Hall?

An unexpected silence told Tom that Kate had run out of things to say about the feast, and Tom was at last able to speak.

"So have you seen anything else?"

She thought for a moment and then said, "There's a huge spider's web on the window near the front door— enormous. I've never seen one so big. And it has two flies stuck in it already. I watched them flapping about trying to escape. And oh, yes. Carew has been in and out of the stables all morning, carrying boxes around. Well, not exactly *around*. More like *into* the stables."

Tom sighed with exasperation. Sometimes his sister just didn't understand what the important things were. According to John Middlemore, Carew wanted to store farming tools in the stables—maybe that's what was in then boxes he'd stumbled over in the passageway? But why was an accountant moving them? Surely he could get some servants to do it?

Before she could ramble on about dresses and food and spiders again, he suggested that they should pay a visit to the stables. Those boxes sounded interesting—maybe they were the ones he'd stumbled over in the passageway?

"In this weather? Oh Tom. They're probably full of food for the big feast."

Kate's voice was peevish and resentful, but she followed him out of the house.

As they set off along the sodden path that led to the stables, Tom caught sight of Carew darting into the old stable block. He carried a large bundle of coarse sacking under his arm. Quickly Tom pulled Kate behind a bush and pressed his finger to his lips, warning her to be silent.

When Carew emerged from the stables, he no longer carried the sacking, and with a furtive glance around, he set off in the opposite direction.

"Come on," whispered Tom urgently. "Let's see what's going on in there."

Kate hesitated briefly, but then followed Tom, who was already at the entrance to the stables.

The children stepped inside and the familiar musky smell of stale straw and horses enveloped them. Everything looked the same as it did the last time they were there. Nothing seemed to be out of place, nothing had moved. And there were no boxes to be seen anywhere, just some torn scraps of paper on the floor.

"Are you sure you saw Carew here?" Tom asked. "You could have been mistaken. It's hard to see in this weather."

He bent down to pick up a scrap of paper and unfolded it carefully with trembling fingers. Both of the children peered intently at it. Tom frowned. There were no words on it at all, just a drawing of a disembodied hand.

"It's a hand!" exclaimed Kate, excitedly.

"No, really?" commented Tom, his voice heavy with sarcasm. "And how did you manage to work that out, Mistress Genius?"

"Well, there's the thumb and four fingers..." began Kate, seemingly unaware of the tone of mockery in Tom's voice.

"Yes, I *can* see," interrupted Tom. "But look here." He pointed to the paper. "That's a nail—a metal nail, not a finger-nail—and these are drops of blood where the nail has punctured the palm of the hand."

Kate stared at the gory image. "Yuk," she said. "That's not very nice, is it?"

"You know what this is, don't you?" said Tom.

Kate shook her head.

"It's one of the Five Wounds of Christ. There's supposed to be two hands and two feet, all bleeding from the wounds caused by the Crucifixion. Don't you pay attention in church?" Tom went on.

"Listen who's talking!" exclaimed Kate, her eyes wide with indignation. "You're always day-dreaming in church. I don't understand it because I'm younger than you. But I can count, and that's only four. What's the fifth wound?"

"Well," said Tom. "Usually it's a bleeding heart, which represents the wound in Jesus' side where the spear went in..." He paused, seeing the expression of disgust on Kate's face turn to one of horror. "But sometimes it's the Crown of Thorns."

He smiled down his nose at Kate, and was congratulating himself on working this out, when she interrupted his thoughts.

"So what does all this stuff mean?"

"What stuff?"

"These notes here—what does it say? 'G & S to take KH. Princess M to London.'

Tom looked at her.

" 'Princess M' could be Princess Mary, King Henry's eldest daughter. And 'KH' could be King Henry..."

An arrow-shaft of panic pierced Tom's body and his heart began to beat faster as he recalled Sir Charles Gerard's words after the search. Could this be the plot he mentioned?

"We need to know what G & S is. Come on, Kate. Let's look round to see if there's any more."

Suddenly, he saw a pile of sacking in the corner of one of the stalls. He gestured to Kate to come with him. Gingerly, they crept forward towards the sacking. As they got closer, it became obvious that the sacking was covering something. Tom knelt down and cautiously lifted one corner of the coarse material and peered under it.

"Boxes," he said briefly, with some satisfaction, and looked up at Kate. "Wooden boxes, all the same."

He pulled the sacking back further to expose some of the boxes. They certainly looked like the ones he'd seen in the passageway, long and narrow. What, he wondered, could possibly fit in such an odd-shaped box? They looked too small to hold farming tools. Carefully, and without making a noise, he inspected the lids of all the boxes, hoping this time to find one which was loose. He was in luck. One of the lids had clearly been nailed down in a hurry, as it was quite loose, and Tom was quick to release it.

What he saw made his heart pound so fiercely he felt as if it would break out of his chest. His legs trembled and his mouth was suddenly dry. For there, glinting in the weak, rain-soaked daylight, were several polished swords, all identical, all unused! Tom realised that these were not the ornamental, jewel-encrusted swords of noblemen, worn to impress others. These were the plain, honed swords of fighting men, viciously sharpened and intended for use in combat!

Tom swallowed hard. Here was danger, real danger! Not some imagined mischief, some long-held grudge against a valued member of his father's staff. This was treason—this *was* the plot to kill the king and put Princess Mary on the throne! What else could it be? With trembling hands, he replaced the lid and covered the deadly boxes with the sacking. Satisfied that the sacking now covered the boxes exactly as it did before, he turned to Kate, who was pale and shaking with terror, took her hand in his, and made hurriedly towards to door of the stables.

"We have to tell Father now!" he hissed. "Quick!"

"And just where do you think you're going?" said a voice from the shadows. Tom turned to see the figure of Carew emerging from the darkness.

How long has he been there? thought Tom, panic-stricken. What has he seen?

"I hope you haven't been poking your nose into things which shouldn't concern you. Because if you have, I'll have to make sure it doesn't happen again," he continued menacingly.

Tom remembered the savage beating that Mary got from Carew, and swallowed hard once more. He pushed Kate behind him protectively, his heart racing wildly.

"If you lay a finger on us..." he began in a high-pitched, reedy voice.

"You'll what?" interrupted Carew. "Tell your father? Tell him what, exactly? That you spend your time in the stables, being careless, leaving doors open so more horses go free?"

"But we didn't," replied Tom, defiantly. "That was one of your friends, wasn't it? And why put the swords here? If the house is searched, they'll be found for sure. And then you'll be…"

"Not me," sneered Carew. "These are your father's stables. So don't think of running off to tell tales. Who'll believe you? Your father certainly won't—not when I've finished with him."

Carew grabbed Tom fiercely by the shoulder of his tunic and pushed his face close to him. His green eyes blazed fiercely and his mouth was contorted into a gargoyle-like grimace. His face and hair were damp from the rain and Tom could see tiny droplets of spit speckling his beard.

"Stay away from me. Stay away from here. Tell no-one what you've seen, or you'll ruin everything. It's time I took back what's rightfully mine, and neither you nor your stupid father can stop me. Very soon, he'll be nothing. And what's more," he added, "once I have what I want, there'll be no loose ends, no witnesses to point the finger at me. So don't think Stockton and Hussey will be around to help you out."

Tom nodded frantically, hoping this would convince him to let them go. This man was surely capable of terrible things, and he had Kate to protect.

But Carew wasn't finished. Still holding Tom by the tunic, he went on, "You're getting into things you don't understand. Your father needs to take you firmly in hand. Now, get out of here and keep your privileged mouth shut, snot-nose!" His voice became a growling whisper, and he released Tom abruptly.

As soon as he realised he was free, Tom turned, grabbed Kate's hand once more and ran, dragging her roughly behind him. The trees, path, bushes all merged into a multicoloured blur as they rushed past.

"Got to get to the Hall!" he gasped. "Tell Father!"

Behind him, Kate stumbled and lurched her way along the path to the Hall, not stopping until their headlong rush brought them breathless into the sanctuary of Sir Richard's study.

"What in the name of…?"

Sir Richard stood up and glared at Tom and Kate— mud-spattered and panting hoarsely, their wet clothes dripping silently onto the polished wooden floor.

"Father! It's Carew! He's the… traitor! He's put boxes…in the stables…"

Sir Richard walked calmly from behind his writing-desk and stood in front of Tom.

"Sir Jacob? A traitor? What feeble nonsense have you dreamed up now, boy?"

Tom winced at his father's sneering voice. At least he had his attention now. He'd make him listen this time. He had to make him listen. Pale flames of anger flickered at the edges of his fear. He breathed in deeply to steady his voice.

"He's been moving boxes to the stables all morning. Boxes of…"

"Yes, I know. I told him to move them there. We can't have them cluttering up the Hall."

Tom's legs shook as the enormity of his father's response dawned on him. He knew? About the swords? And the plot? Was his father a traitor too?

No. Never. Surely not!

"But...they're full of..."

"Ploughshares. Yes, I know. I told him to store them there—convenient if we need to use them. We lost most of our stock in that damnable barn fire."

Ploughshares? What lies had Carew spun to cover up his treachery? Tom felt sick to his stomach. How could his father have been so duped by this evil man?

"No, Father. They're swords, not ploughshares!"

Sir Richard stared at him for so long without blinking that Tom wondered if he'd been struck dumb by some ancient spell. His jaw moved up and down for several seconds before he could utter a sound.

"Swords? In my stables? I doubt it very much."

"Father, we've seen them. Boxes and boxes of them."

The need to tell his father, to make him believe, was overwhelming. He was about to continue when Sir Richard held up his hand firmly.

"Well, we shall see for ourselves then. But if you are lying then you know the consequences."

He strode over to the door, opened it and called imperiously, "Carew! Bring me one of those boxes from the stables, please. Now!"

He walked back to his writing-desk and sat down.

Seconds passed like hours before the door opened once more and Carew came in carrying one of the boxes.

"Set it down here, Carew, and let's see what's inside. The Good Lord knows these have cost me enough—I'd like to see what I'm paying for."

Carew shot Tom a sideways glance before setting then box down on the floor. Taking a small knife from his pocket, he slid it firmly under the lid and twisted it sharply. The lid came away easily. Tom held his breath, his heart pounding. The flame of victory began to burn fiercely in his chest, like the glory beacons of the King's battles. Now you'll get what's coming to you! Now my father will know you for what you are!

The lid clattered on the oaken floor and Tom stared down, eagerly anticipating his success.

But instead of the sharp greyness of the swords, Tom saw the dull iron of three new ploughshares! His eyes widened in disbelief. How had he done that?

Sir Richard nodded curtly to Carew.

"Thank you. Now you can put this with the others."

Carew bowed, and turned to leave. But as he did so, he glanced once more at Tom. His eyes shone with the unmistakeable gleam of triumph.

"Tom, this has to stop, now. Sir Jacob is an honest, hard-working accountant. He has my absolute trust and authority and I will not have you inventing malicious and dangerous lies about him. Do you understand?" Sir Richard's voice was clipped and ice cold.

Tom nodded miserably. At least his father didn't

know about the plot. That was some relief. Once more Carew had fooled him. If only he would listen—just to come to the stables and see for himself?

But his father was still speaking.

"You seem to be waging some childish vendetta against him, ever since that Fishwyck incident all those months ago. I thought I made it clear then that any contact with Papist rebels like them was both dangerous and forbidden. He reported your conduct to me, which was fit and proper. He came to us highly recommended by his previous employers. The Sheriff himself wrote a glowing commendation of him."

"But..."

"No, Tom. Your conduct has given me grave cause for concern for some time. You are old enough to know the difference between right and wrong. You are not a child any more and already you have acquired a reputation in the village for mischief."

Tom opened his mouth to interrupt, but one glance from his father's basilisk eyes made him close it sharply.

"Do I have to remind you of that unpleasantness last year with Widow Hamer's washing?" continued Sir Richard. "Now, no more of this nonsense. Look at the state of your sister."

Tom turned to look at Kate. He gown was streaked with wet patches and her hair hung in damp tendrils over her shoulders.

"If she has caught her death because of your stupidity, I will make sure you bear the guilt for the rest of your life.

Now get out of my sight!"

Tom clasped Kate's hand tight and trembling, led her out of the study to the warmth of his bed-chamber. She squeezed his hand firmly in response. A thin haze of steam rose from her damp clothes, making her look even more waif-like.

"I'm frightened, Tom."

He put his arm clumsily around her shoulder.

"What should we do now?" Kate's voice trembled and her eyes brimmed with tears as she looked up at him.

"I don't know, Kate. I just don't know."

Who could he tell? Who could he trust? His father had been completely taken in by Carew's treachery and wickedness. His mother would surely take his father's side—she always did. The servants? What could they do?

"We have to stop them on our own, Kate."

Tom's jaw was set firm and his voice was unwavering.

"Tomorrow it's the Fair and Edward will be waiting. If Father won't listen to us, I'll find someone who will."

Folio XI

Tom watched unmoving as the bright dawn spread like a golden veil over the Haswell estate. Every sinew, every bone in his body ached with sleeplessness. How long had he been awake? It felt like he'd wrestled all night with his bedcovers, seeking out each cool patch of linen in an effort to find sleep. Each slow, dark minute felt like an hour, but now the minutes would not pass quickly enough. Today was the day Edward had promised to meet him at the Fair. Maybe he would know someone who would help them stop Carew?

"Tom! Tom! Are you awake? It's a lovely day today. The sun's shining, the guests are awake and we have so much to do."

Tom's stomach leapt in panic. What if she wanted him to stay here and help?

He padded quickly back to his bed and lay quite still, trying to imitate the shallow breathing of a sleeper. Maybe he could persuade her that they should be out of the way today? The door opened and Tom heard his mother's swishing skirts as she walked over to his bed.

Lady Haswell sat on the edge of Tom's bed and ruffled his hair affectionately. Yawning loudly, he rubbed his eyes and looked up at her. She was an older version of Kate, almost a carbon copy, and for the first time in his life, Tom was aware of how beautiful his mother was. Her hair was fair and golden, like Kate's, but whereas Kate's was allowed to hang freely, hers was pinned up in elaborate coils and covered by a jewelled gabled headdress and hood, which shimmered in the early morning sunlight. Her damask kirtle and taffeta gown rustled gently as she moved, and the dark red fabric contrasted vividly with the pale radiance of her skin.

"Breakfast first, then your horses need exercising. You can go to the fair in Myersford. Your father and I have a lot to attend to here."

Tom's heart almost sang with relief. What a stroke of good fortune! She actually wanted him to go to the Fair!

He clambered out of bed quickly and reached out for the clothes his mother had laid out for him. In contrast with his ordinary russet doublet, a fine new burgundy one with full breeches was lying on the chair in his bed-chamber. A delicate linen shirt with lace cuffs lay next to it. Tom glared at the expensive garments, hating every thread of them.

"If we're riding to the fair, wouldn't it be better to keep these for the feast tonight? I'd hate to get them muddy."

And I don't fancy walking round the village looking

like some Spanish lady's maid, either, he thought.

His mother looked at him and laughed. "Don't be silly. These aren't your clothes for tonight. You don't think I'd send you out in your very best clothes, do you?" she said, lightly. Then her tone became more serious.

"It's important that you look your best in public today. There are important people visiting and your father wants to make a good impression—and that means you have to do your bit too."

"Why? Is it those friends of Carew's?" Tom's cheeks burned hot as he thought of how his father was making such a blatant effort to please these strangers. A little butterfly of anxiety fluttered in his chest as he recalled Carew's threats of the previous day. His loathing for the man burned inside him like a Midsummer beacon.

"Yes, it is Sir Jacob's friends."

She emphasised his name and frowned at Tom. "They have the ear of the King, and the rumour is that there will be some new titles created by him soon—earls or baronets, perhaps." Lady Haswell smiled wistfully.

"I know it's hard work, Tom, and we've had enough to deal with lately, but it could make a big difference to all our lives. I mean, a baronet, Tom. That really would be something. Now hurry up. Kate's already downstairs."

She swept gracefully out of the room and closed the door behind her.

Once again Tom's fears shrouded him. Carew's wicked plotting was obvious; the visits to the stables, the priest's robe, the swords and the papers—it all made sense now. Carew was plotting a rebellion and using Myersford as his base! But why? What was so special about Myersford?

He pulled his clothes on and headed downstairs, glancing at the freshly-painted portraits of his mother and father as he went. Stupid man! Why wouldn't he listen?

Suddenly, he stopped. Hadn't Carew said that? That his father was stupid? What were his words? *'It's time I took back what's rightfully mine...'* What did he mean?

"Tom! Hurry up!"

Kate's voice echoed up the staircase.

"The horses are saddled and waiting for us," she said, "so eat up quickly and we can get to the fair."

Tom grabbed a hunk of bread and stuffed it in his pocket.

"I'm not really hungry," he explained. "I'll keep it for later."

They ran outside into the early morning sunshine. A shimmering veil of dew glistened on the elegantly manicured lawns which spread out in front of Lower Myersford Hall, and the scent of the summer flowers hung in the light air. John Middlemore was standing between two horses, holding each by the reins. One of them tossed its head and snorted impatiently.

"Good morning, Master Tom, Mistress Kate," he said, amicably, and nodded respectfully to them.

Soon, the children were trotting along down the main street of Myersford. There was an air of expectancy in the village, a liveliness and a sense of excited pleasure that

Tom couldn't share. The street through the village was a sea of colour with flowers and twisted straw decorations hanging from every low-slung roof.

Tom and Kate dismounted and led their horses slowly through the busy crowd of people to Harry Wiswall's smithy. As he walked along the winding path to the stabling area, he heard someone softly calling his name. He looked up and saw Mary's face smiling at him from the doorway.

"What are you doing here?"

"Working, of course. Mr Middlemore fixed it for me. He found me and brought me here. I help Mr Wiswall with the horses now."

Tom looked at her cheery face. The swelling that was there before had almost gone, and the bruises that remained could pass for dirt. And now she could spend more time with the horses she loved so much.

"Middlemore? He found you?" Tom asked.

"Yes. He brought me here and Mistress Wiswall looked after me," she replied. "Thanks for helping me. I don't know what I'd've done if you hadn't."

"We were really worried when you disappeared," said Kate. "We thought something terrible had happened to you."

"Yes, you might have told us."

Tom frowned at her. Although he now knew how Mary had come to be with the Wiswalls, he still felt aggrieved. Surely she could have sent a message, or John could have told them?

"Why all the secrecy? If we'd known where you were, we'd have visited you."

"I didn't think you'd be concerned. After all, I'm not even a servant any more. Just another nobody. And I've a lot to do here. Most of the time I'm here with the horses. That one over there's had the colic and I've had to walk him most nights."

She pointed to a tired-looking creature in the corner of the stable.

"But come over here. I have some news for you."

Mary led them to a sheltered spot, away from the road.

"Two nights ago," she began, "I saw summat strange in the village. Just down the street yonder."

Tom's heart quickened its pace and he moved a little closer.

"Like I said, I were walking him round the stable when I saw a shadow flitting around. I reckon it's that priest they're looking for."

"How do you know it was a priest? It could have been anyone—a thief maybe."

"No, I'm certain it were a priest. There were a death in that house there, a baby, newborn. And that's where I saw him. He come out of the house, made the sign of the cross, and I heard a voice say, 'Thank you, Father'. I think he were called to baptise the child so the Devil couldn't claim its soul. Baby were buried the next day."

Tom whistled softly.

"So he's still here, is he? Did you tell anyone?"

"No. Thought I'd best tell you first. And there's more."

Mary paused a moment before continuing.

"Those friends of Sir Jacob—I know their names. Sir Neville Hussey and John Stockton."

A sudden clatter of hooves on the road behind them distracted Mary and she turned to see three more horses being led into the stable.

"I have to go. I'll see you soon."

Tom and Kate waved their goodbyes.

"I've never heard of them, have you?" said Tom. "Maybe Edward knows them. Come on."

They set off towards the centre of the village. Tom was certain that Edward would be in the same place as on Market Day. He was right. Edward *was* in the same place.

"Look at you."

Edward grinned and plucked gently at Tom's new doublet. Tom grinned back, then sat down next to him. Kate did the same.

"Listen," he said, unable to contain himself any longer, "we've got some news."

Edward listened in silence to Tom's account of Carew's activities in the stables and the strange piece of paper they'd picked up at the hunt. He gave no flicker of recognition when Tom named Carew's friends. Not once did he interrupt, but his face showed concern when Tom recounted the accountant's threats.

"That explains something that's been puzzling me," he said.

"What?" asked Kate.

"Well," began Edward. "Since my father was—taken—we've learnt to listen to rumour and gossip. People of our…beliefs have to be careful. Keep your nose clean, watch your back and keep your eyes and ears open. You find out very quickly who your friends are, who you can trust. And sometimes you learn things that keep you out of trouble's way. I've also learned that a man's religion shouldn't really matter. Whether he's for King Harry or the Bishop of Rome, all that counts is whether he's a good neighbour—if he keeps his estate well, pays his servants on time, cares for his family—not what happens on Sundays. Do you remember when people went on a pilgrimage to Rome, or Canterbury or Compostela, to see a shrine or holy relic?" asked Edward.

"Yes," replied Tom, puzzled. Edward's sudden change of topic caught him unawares. He'd forgotten how Edward's mind could flash from one subject to another with lightning speed.

"How did you know they'd been on a pilgrimage?"

"Because they wore a little badge like, oh, palm leaves if they'd been to Jerusalem." Tom remembered seeing people with pilgrim badges, which they wore like prized trophies.

"Well," went on Edward. "There are some people around Langford who wear the badge of the Five Wounds of Christ, a bit like a pilgrim would."

"So where have they been?" asked Kate, suddenly curious.

"Well, that's what puzzles me," said Edward. "Nowhere, as far as I can make out. It's almost as if they're planning to go on a pilgrimage and they're wearing the badge before they get there."

Tom thought deeply about this for several moments. "What kind of pilgrimage needs swords, Edward? Because if we're right, and Carew and his friends are planning something, it's going to happen at Midsummer—which is today. What can we do, Edward?"

Edward's reply was instant.

"I think we need to tell someone about all this. It's too serious for us to meddle with. You could be—no, you *are*—in real danger. There's treason here, I'm sure of it. I know Papists—God's Blood, I'm one of them—but I wouldn't see you or your family suffer, Tom. We were, are, good friends and that counts above all else."

He put a reassuring hand on Tom's shoulder. Unflinching, he looked directly into his eyes. Tom felt a wave of despair engulf him.

"I've tried, Edward. I went to my father yesterday but he wouldn't listen. He believes everything Carew tells him. The man's been using our money too, I'm sure of it. Stealing from the accounts... and I just don't know who to tell..."

Tom sniffed and forced back the tears that threatened to betray his fears. Edward looked at him. His voice was low and steady, and there was a kindness in it which lifted Tom's spirits.

"There is one person you could go to, and I know he

would help you."

"Who?"

"Harry Wiswall, the Constable. He can go to the Sheriff—tell him everything. He'll know what to do."

Tom shivered. The sun had disappeared and a chill was in the air. Above, the white bank of cloud was turning darker, and there was an oppressive stillness all around. Harry Wiswall was a pleasant enough man, he thought, but would he believe him? There was that incident last summer with Widow Winnard's cat…The Constable hadn't been quite so pleasant towards him then. But this was different. He got to his feet decisively. "We'll do it," he said curtly. "Now."

Abruptly, he turned and set off with a determined stride in the direction of Wiswall's smithy, stumbling over the dry, dusty street, with the others following close behind.

Folio XII

Harry Wiswall was sitting on a low wall by his yard. A shining film of sweat covered his brow, and his face was even more ruddy than usual. Wearily, he picked up a cloth and wiped his face and shoulders, all the while talking to someone who was only partially visible. As Tom rounded the corner, the Someone came into view. It was John Middlemore.

The groom was talking animatedly to Harry. Gesticulating wildly with his hands; he seemed to be telling him something, for Harry nodded, as if agreeing with him. Tom moved closer slowly until he was within earshot. He stopped and motioned the others to stay back. The men's conversation was inaudible, dulled by the heavy summer air.

What if Middlemore is part of plot? he thought. I can hardly tell Harry in front of him. Maybe I should wait? His lungs ached with the effort of running and he swallowed hard to regain some normality.

He was about to turn away, to bide his time until

Middlemore left when suddenly the groom looked up

"Now, Master Tom. What's happening with you today?"

Middlemore's voice was warm and cheerful.

"And Master Edward? Why I didn't know you two were still…"

His voice tailed off as Edward and Kate joined him, still breathless from their desperate rush across the village.

"Whatever's happened? Your sister looks quite poorly."

Mary came out of the stables and smiled warmly at them. But it soon faded when she saw the anguish which was etched plainly on Kate's face.

Tom sank down on the wall by the Constable hoping to regain his breath. His chest burned with the effort of running and deep in his skull a hammer pounded incessantly. The men waited patiently for him to speak, concern visible in their faces.

"Out with it, lad," urged Middlemore, his deep voice warm with concern.

"Tell him," panted Edward. "You must. You can trust him—I *know*."

Tom breathed in deeply; the burden of his worries was now too much to bear. Harry Wiswall was no fool. He wouldn't associate with anyone who might be a traitor, would he? And Middlemore had shown kindness to Mary.

"There's a plot to kill the King!" he blurted out. "And Carew's involved. You have to stop him. He's got swords up at the Hall, hidden in the stables, and it's going to happen tonight…"

"Calm down, lad. Calm down."

The Constable's quiet voice was instantly reassuring. Tom sat down and waited until the pounding hammer had diminished to a persistent throbbing.

"Carew has been carrying boxes to the stables all morning, boxes of swords!" He paused to gather his thoughts. "And we found bits of paper that mention taking Princess Mary to London…"

"Carew!" Middlemore spat vehemently into a mound of straw by the road. "That woodlouse! What does he know about anything? Fancies himself as some fine horse expert, but he doesn't know dung from a dormouse!"

Then he grabbed Harry's arm eagerly. "Didn't I tell you there was something strange about him?"

Tom stared. Did Middlemore already know about this? How? The groom turned to the three children.

"I found the boxes this morning and saw something metal in one of them. Thought it was those tools he was talking about. Carew was doing his usual snooping so I couldn't see much else. Didn't see no papers though. What exactly was on them?"

His eyes narrowed and he looked piercingly at Tom.

"Horrible pictures," said Kate. "Bleeding hands and nails. The sort of thing that gives you nightmares."

"It's the Five Wounds," explained Edward. "Like the badge those people in Langford wear on their cloaks."

Middlemore nodded. "But what did the bits of paper

say. You said something about Princess Mary?"

Tom concentrated hard to recall the exact wording.

" '*G & S to take KH. Princess M to London.*' And we thought maybe this meant that someone was planning to take Princess Mary to London to replace the King, just like the Sheriff said. But we don't know what the G & S bit means."

He looked enquiringly at the groom, hoping for an answer. When none came, he continued.

"Then Carew found us in the stables."

A sudden glint of concern appeared in Middlemore's eyes, but he said nothing.

"He threatened us, said something about taking what was rightfully his and that no-one would believe us if we told anyone. I tried to tell Father, but Carew fooled him by showing him a box that really did have ploughshares in. You do believe me, don't you?"

For a brief moment, a bleak veil of doubt enveloped him. What if John and Harry thought he was making it up? They were his last hope.

But neither man made any response; Tom resumed his tale and played his trump card.

"And when I told him about the priest's robe, he more or less said I'd made it up."

Tom sat, shoulders hunched, and stared despondently at the rutted track of the street. His legs felt heavy, like lead, and the pounding in his head had started again. The air was so thick with moisture he could hardly breathe.

"What priest's robe?"

Harry Wiswall's voice cut through the oppressive air like a dagger through a velvet curtain.

"I found it in the stables when I were sleeping there." Everyone turned to look at Mary, who was standing awkwardly at the side. "I used it to keep warm. A sort of grey colour, it were."

Harry nodded.

"Ay, like as not it's one of the White Monks' robes." He looked at Tom, the admiration plain on his face. "It looks like you're right, Master Thomas. It's a plot all right. And a costly one at that. Who's paying for all this? That's what I'd like to know. Who's behind it?"

A trickle of sweat ran down from his temple and he wiped his brow once more. Tom stared at the Constable, hardly daring to breathe. They believed him! So there was still a chance to save his family, to save Myersford!

Harry turned to Middlemore and raised his eyebrow, a subtle movement but the groom responded to its unspoken question.

"No, I don't believe it's Sir Richard. Sure enough, he has the riches to pay for it, but I've seen nothing that says he's a traitor. He's a loyal supporter of the King."

A thunderbolt of knowledge suddenly struck home. Of course! That's it! It has to be! That's what I've been missing all along!

"It's Carew again! He's been stealing from my father. I heard them talking about some money that's missing from the accounts. He must have used some of it to pay for the weapons—and now it looks like my father's done it! We have to stop them."

His voice became a weak, barely audible croak, and his mouth was dry with terror. John Middlemore sat down on the wall next to Tom and spoke calmly.

"I think you're right, young Tom. Sweet Jesus, you've a wit that would cut through winter butter. It must have been the priest that let the horses loose—maybe accidentally—and poor Mary took a beating for it. Carew must have hidden him in the stables. Your father is a good man, Tom, but he is also ambitious and naïve—he can't tell good from evil. And that's dangerous in these troubled times."

Gently he put his arm around Tom's shoulder.

"Harry and I, we'll go to the Sheriff at first light tomorrow…"

"But it's going to happen tonight, at Midsummer!" shouted Kate. "We heard them in the stables. You've got to stop them today!"

Harry spread his hands helplessly.

"The Sheriff's in Lancaster. It'll be a good few hours before I can get there, and you see how I'm fixed here. The whole village and more besides are here for the Fair."

"I can look after things here, Mr Wiswall." Mary's quiet, calm voice gave hope once more to Tom.

John thought for a moment.

"Listen, this might work. Harry, if you go to the Sheriff and tell him to come to Myersford, Tom and I can hold them until you get there. We can do that, can't we, Tom?"

John Middlemore's piercing grey eyes were wide and pleading. Tom hesitated. Carew and his men were dangerous and this plan was not without its risks. What if they were too late and the men had already left for London? Tom stiffened his shoulders, bracing himself for the uncertainty that lay ahead. The groom's calm assertiveness and quiet confidence was infectious. With this man to help and advise him, there was nothing he couldn't, or wouldn't do to save his family.

"Tell me what I have to do," he said firmly. "Tell me, and I'll do it."

The children clustered around and listened in silence as Middlemore set out his plans.

"Harry, you get that message to the Sheriff. He needs to know Carew is the traitor. Then get some men from the village. If the plotters decide to make a run for it, we'll be ready. Mary, you stay here so Harry can set off as soon as possible. When the village is quiet, lock up and go home— there's no need to put yourself in danger."

He turned to Tom and Kate.

"Now, you two. If it's to be tonight, then it will be at the Feast. We have to do this carefully so that your father comes out of this without any suspicion. I won't be in the Great Hall tonight. But you will, and I need you to watch those two-faced dogs for me."

Tom looked up at him. "You mean, those friends of Carew's?"

"I do indeed. Watch them, and tell me when they leave—I'll be waiting outside in the kitchen garden, and

Harry and his men will be waiting down the road to arrest them if they leave. The Sheriff will already know what's going on."

Then Middlemore turned to Edward who had remained quiet through all this.

"You should stay well away from the Hall tonight. We can't have you lurking around if it's a matter of treason." He smiled. "You of all people should know why this is important."

Edward made the slightest of smiles in return, almost imperceptible. Tom's mind reeled. What hidden knowledge was here? More secrets?

Middlemore looked keenly at Tom. A half-smile played along his lips.

"You remember when we met in the churchyard that Sunday?"

Tom nodded.

"It was my brother's grave I was visiting. That mound of earth, unmarked, along with all the paupers, is the last resting place of Francis Middlemore—Father Francis Middlemore. This is all I have to remember him by."

A gentle breeze whipped up the dust from the road, and a swirl of grit skittered against the wall. Middlemore reached inside his shirt and pulled out something bright and gleaming—a finely wrought golden chain, with tiny beads of black jet separating the links at intervals. It shimmered delicately, like fine lace as the light caught them. And looped on the end of the Rosary was a cross bearing the figure of a crucified man.

"He was a priest?" Tom's voice was incredulous. "But that means you're a …."

"Papist? A heretic?" Middlemore smiled warmly at him. "I suppose I am."

"But you were in church, and…"

Tom searched vainly for words that would not come. So he was right! Their own groom was a Papist! But how could this be?

Edward laid a friendly hand on his arm.

"It's like I said, Tom. A man's religion doesn't really matter; it's his deeds that count. Not all Papists are traitors."

"And not all traitors are Papists."

A cautious tone crept into Middlemore's voice. "When my brother met his end on the gallows at Tyburn, I realised that life was precious, more precious than anything, for as long as we are alive, we have hope of a better future. My future lay here, in Lancashire, where men are judged by their deeds and not their religion. Many assumed I would want to avenge my brother's death. They were wrong. All I want is a peaceful life, with a roof over my head and food on the table. And thanks to your father, that's what I have. I thought once to follow Francis into the priesthood but my real love is horses."

He indicated his leather boots.

"His last gift to me."

"What happened to him?" Kate's tentative voice could barely be heard.

Middlemore's reply was firm and decisive.

"My brother was fooled by agents of the king and paid the same price as many before him. I don't want to end my days at the end of a gibbet, hanging like a rotten piece of meat for all to see. So I keep my nose clean, go to church as the law demands and serve my master, your father. And in the private church of my heart and mind, my beliefs are my business. And now you must watch those lying traitors, so we can catch them red-handed."

So Edward was right; John *was* a good man. Not a thief, or a traitor as he'd feared.

Tom steeled himself for the task ahead. If he did nothing, the king would die. And if the plot were traced back to Myersford, and his father implicated, the hangman's noose would claim yet more innocent victims. Carew would win.

"Kate and I will watch them and when they make their move, one of us will come and find you," he said.

"What happens then?" asked Kate. "Are you going to...kill them?"

"That's not for us to do," replied Harry Wiswall. "If they come quietly, they'll be kept under lock and key, then sent to Lancaster Castle for trial."

Kate sighed, relieved by his answer. Tom turned to her. "We need to go," he said. "There's a lot to do at home. Until tonight, then."

"Until tonight," rejoined the groom. "Pray that the Good Lord bless our work, for the lives of many depend on it."

Pray indeed, he thought, for the deeds of evil men are truly wicked. Once more Tom felt his fear rising in his throat, and a trembling pulse beat rapidly in his temple. If they failed tonight, all their lives would change for ever.

Folio XIII

A heavy gloom hung over the sultry, humid Midsummer day. Even the gathering crowds of villagers, intent on spending a holiday in merrymaking and jollity, did not stir any excitement in Tom's heart. He walked along the street, his stomach griping with worry. What if it all went wrong and Carew escaped? Or if the Sheriff didn't get there in time?

All around him people jostled and pushed in their eagerness to get to the Fair. Kate held Tom's arm tightly as they made their way to the village boundary. Edward lagged behind, cut off from them by the scurrying crowd.

Then, as Tom wove through the mass of people, he caught sight of something that made his pulse race. A flash of gold and crimson silk, a patch of glinting fabric half-hidden by crowd. Tom moved his head slightly to make sure. There it was again, the expensive cloth of gold so out of place in the swaying mass of villagers.

Suddenly he stumbled, distracted by a small child crawling near his feet, and in an instant the man disappeared from view. Damn him! he thought. Where is he now? Where's he gone?

Once more the crowd shifted and Tom had a clear view of his quarry. No, he wasn't mistaken. It *was* Carew, engrossed in conversation with another man whose face he couldn't see. He stopped dead.

"What are you staring at?"

Edward's voice was barely audible above the roar of the cheering crowd. Tom pointed across the street.

"That's Carew, over there."

"Where?"

Edward stared hard in the direction Tom was pointing.

"There in the red and gold doublet, talking to that other man. That's Carew!"

Edward stared without moving a muscle, without uttering a sound for so long that Tom began to wonder if the apoplexy had struck him.

"Edward? What is it? Do you know him?"

He tapped gently on his arm. Edward leant close to Tom, keeping his eyes fixed on Carew and his companion.

"Oh, yes," he whispered. "I know him all right, but he's not Sir Jacob Carew. In fact, he's not Sir Anybody— not any more."

The raucous cheers of the crowd faded from Tom's ears and for a brief second it was as if all time was suspended. He could barely speak. An invisible noose of anxiety tightened around his throat.

"So who is he then?"

Despite the hubbub around them, Tom heard nothing but Edward's reply.

"Jacob Glover."

"Who?"

Tom had never heard of him, he was sure of that. So why did his name strike such a chord of recognition?

"One of the Langford Glovers," continued Edward. "He hasn't been seen or heard of for years. I thought he was in jail—or worse!"

His voice was quiet, and when he finally looked at Tom, his eyes were dark with concern.

"Jacob Glover was ruthless in the pursuit of money, but he didn't like the hard work that went with it. He gambled, drank, stole—did anything that got him riches the easy way. Almost bankrupted his family, and then abandoned them when the King's Commissioners came."

Tom gazed fixedly at the rutted path, seeing nothing. His mind was distracted by a dim fragment of memory, a recollection of John Middlemore speaking affectionately of Lady Margaret Stanley, whose father was Sir William Glover of Langford. And of a brother who broke his heart. Could it possibly be? Could Jacob Glover and Margaret Stanley's wayward brother be one and the same?

"Edward, did he have a sister Margaret who married into the Stanleys of Myersford?"

"Yes, I think he did. Why?"

Edward's eyes were dark with curiosity.

Tom breathed in deeply to the fullest extent of his lungs. His stomach churned and his heart beat uncontrollably against his ribs. Above him the sky lightened briefly, as if the sun was about to break through the damp heavy air, but almost at once the grey clouds regrouped and the oppressiveness returned. Another memory, this time of Carew in the stables, whispering conspiratorially to his unknown friend. He turned to Kate.

"What were those names Mary gave you? Carew's friends?"

His tone was low and urgent. Kate looked up at him in surprise. She screwed her eyes up as she thought.

"Hussey and Stockton, wasn't it?"

"Hell's Breath! That's it!" he exclaimed. "G & S—it must be Glover and Stockton. They're the G and S on the note."

Edward suddenly grabbed Tom's arm, his eyes bright with triumph.

"It must be Glover and Stockton who are going to kill the King, at Midsummer."

Tom nodded his agreement. Kate hugged him and smiled up at them both.

"So nothing's going to happen tonight and the feast will be wonderful."

Tom gaped in bewilderment and Edward frowned, a deep cleft appearing in his forehead.

"Why do you say that?"

"Because the King's not in Lancashire and they are. So they can't kill him, can they?"

Suddenly Tom knew! About the plot, the papers,

about Midsummer—everything! He knew what Carew was plotting, and why he was doing it. This wasn't about the King, or Princess Mary at all. It wasn't even about the priest. Why hadn't he seen it before? The fancy clothes, the missing money—it all made sense now.

Tom looked at his sister's upturned face, bright and shining with happiness. How could he tell her that in her young innocent chatter she had once more exposed the reality of Carew's cruel treachery?

"You're right, Kate," he muttered. "They can't kill him at Midsummer. Maybe they're not going to kill him at all."

"What?"

The furrow in Edward's forehead deepened as he stared at his friend. "But what about the bits of paper and the secret signs?"

Tom glared once more across at Carew as the vivid recollection of their encounter in the stables flashed into his mind. By now the crowd had thinned and for the first time Carew's friend was clearly visible. Tom watched as Carew handed over some scraps of paper.

" '*It's time I took back what's rightfully mine*'. That's what he said—'*what's rightfully mine*'. It's Myersford!" he said, his voice a deep whisper in the heavy summer air. "That's what he wants—Myersford Hall! He thinks he's entitled to it—his ancestral home, claimed through his sister's marriage to the Stanleys. He wants it for himself— after we've been thrown out onto the street—or worse!"

Kate let out a quiet gasp of anguish. Edward

swallowed hard, his face pale with fear.

"And the plot to kill the King? And the priest?"

"It's just a smokescreen, a trick. If people believe there's a plot, that's enough for us to lose Myersford. The robe, the bits of paper, all planted there by Carew. "

Edward put his arm around Tom's shoulder.

"It won't happen, Tom. John will stop him, and catch the men. And Harry will bring the Sheriff from Lancaster. You'll see. It'll work out in the end."

Tom's mouth was dry and his throat was tight with tension.

"No, Edward. It will happen. Harry won't bring the Sheriff from Lancaster, and Carew and his friends will get clean away."

"How do you know that? How can you be so sure?"

Tom pointed once more at Carew and his friend.

"Because the Sheriff isn't in Lancaster. He's here, in Myersford, talking to his friend, Carew!"

Edward and Kate looked across at the two men. On the other side of the valley, there was a low rumble of thunder, as if a restless giant had just awakened from a bad dream.

Folio XIV

As Tom looked around the Great Hall at Lower Myersford, he felt a thrill of excitement and anticipation run along his spine, like a ghost's bony fingers. Fat white candles sputtered in their sconces, casting a warm yellow glow over the room. Colourful Flemish tapestries hung from the walls, their rich colours contrasting vividly with the brilliance of the long dining tables, on which lay the finest silver cutlery and plates. In the centre of the top table was the centrepiece—a boar's head covered in soot and pig's grease. In a corner of the room a small band of musicians played, as the guests, all dressed in their finery, feasted hungrily on the lavish banquet. It was an impressive and ordered sight, and one which made Tom feel both proud and humble. But he also knew that if Carew (or Glover, or whatever he called himself) succeeded, then their lives would never be the same again.

Tom and Kate were seated at the top table. From this vantage point, they could see almost everything and everybody in the room. Carew and his guests were seated together a short distance away. Nothing seemed out of the ordinary.

As the feasting came to an end and the tables were cleared to make way for the dancing, Tom felt uneasy. It wouldn't be quite so simple to watch his prey now. The guests were already milling around in small groups, and if he followed the men round too closely, they were sure to spot him. Casually, Tom wandered round trying to imitate his father, who was in the best of moods and talking amiably with all the guests.

Carew and his friends were talking quietly together and seemed to have settled themselves close to the musicians. Tom glanced round to see where Kate was. He saw her with his mother, watching him. She smiled and waved to him—it was their secret signal.

Tom turned his attention back to the men, who were still standing by the wall, listening to the musicians. But with one exception—now there was only Carew. Tom's heart leapt and began to beat erratically. Where were the others? Stockton and Hussey? Where had they gone? He looked around sharply, but the men were nowhere to be seen. In a dilemma of indecision, Tom stood rooted to the spot. Should he search for them? Tell John? Stay and watch?

It was Kate who supplied the answer. He saw her come skipping towards him, weaving through the clusters of guests.

"Anything happened?" she whispered eagerly.

"Yes. Hussey and Stockton have left. Stay here and

watch Carew. I'll go and tell John."

Reluctantly, Tom walked to the door that led to the kitchens. I hope Kate is safe, he thought. She doesn't seem to realise the danger we're in; it's just a big adventure to her, a game almost.

He slipped unnoticed through the kitchens and out into the vegetable garden. Nearby a pig grunted disapprovingly.

"John? Are you there?"

Tom's words hung still in the silence. No response.

"John?" Still no response.

Tom began to feel the fear rising in his throat. What had happened? Where was he?

Then in the distance, Tom saw a shadowy figure running across the lawns, heading for the stables. It looked like Hussey. Without thinking, he set off in pursuit, his heart beating fast. The man darted silently down the path in the direction of the stables. The gravel path, illuminated by the moonlight, spread before him like a pale purple ribbon. Tom followed him, all the time keeping to the shaded patches of the garden. There was no sign of the other man, Stockton. Where was he? Already at the stables perhaps?

Suddenly, the man stopped and stood, unmoving. He seemed to be listening. Tom did the same, hardly daring to take breath lest he make a sound and betray his whereabouts. Every fibre of his being was taut, tense, straining to hear every noise, every night time insect. The pale silver shimmer of the moon's light cast a ghostly glow over the lawns. Small bushes were transformed into terrible monsters, and every shadow contained a threat.

Then Tom heard it too; from the direction of the stables came the shouts of men which broke the still darkness of the summer night. He sneaked silently behind a bush and watched closely. What now? It was too far to run back to the house and raise the alarm. John was nowhere to be seen. Maybe he could...

"Got you, you whelp of treachery!"

Tom was held in an iron grip, his arms pinned behind his back, his head forced back as an unseen hand tore his hair from his scalp.

"Thought you could betray us to the Constable, eh? When they find you drowned in the cess-pit, they'll learn not to interfere."

His attacker's foul breath made Tom's stomach churn. Tom cursed silently. What a fool! How could he not have heard the other man creeping up on him? Suddenly Carew was there, sword in hand.

"Enough, Stockton. If we're to risk hanging, let it be for Rome, not child-murder. We have work to do—and fast." Carew's voice was husky with impatience.

"The Sheriff's men are already searching the stables— we must go quickly. Leave the rest of the swords and meet me at Glebe's Corner. I've arranged safe passage to Spain. Once we're aboard the ship, this insignificant worm will trouble us no more."

Stockton stared at him, his pale, narrow lips stretched tight across his decaying teeth.

"Then, our work will continue," he hissed. "Queen Catherine will be avenged when Princess Mary is crowned."

So he's fooled you too, has he? thought Tom. How many people had Carew used to satisfy his greed? How many had he ensnared in his web?

Tom felt his hands tied roughly together, and Stockton then pushed him to the ground. The odour of freshly cut grass invaded his nostrils and made his nose itch. In the distance, the clatter of horses' hooves could be heard. The third man, Hussey, was the first to react.

"Come on, quick. Let's load up and go, before we're missed."

He leaped nimbly onto his horse.

"Catch us up, Carew. Come on, Stockton—now! Leave those there."

Stockton did likewise and the two men left hurriedly, leaving Tom alone with Carew.

What will happen to me now? he thought. If they leave me here, someone will find me soon. At least I'll be alive. But as for Myersford...?

The sound of running feet disturbed his thoughts.

"Hold it there, Carew. There's a noose waiting at Tyburn for you."

It was John Middlemore, flushed, breathless, his sword glinting dangerously.

"If you've harmed the lad, by Jesu, you'll feel the point of my sword now."

Carew smiled arrogantly. "You think your

swordsmanship is better than mine, groom? I doubt it. But let's see what you can do."

He raised his sword and slashed at Middlemore, who parried and then lunged at him. A streak of dark red appeared through Carew's costly satin doublet.

"First blood to me, you aristocratic piece of dung." Middlemore's voice was cold and harsh. "It's your kind who caused my brother's death, with your plots and heresy, duping innocent men, good men, into treason."

Carew laughed, a high cackling laugh like a demonic wolf howling on a storm-filled night.

"You'll be out of a job soon enough when the Sheriff finds the swords. I've made sure he knows exactly where to find them, the proof he needs—not that he needed much encouragement. He's hated Haswell for years. He was more than eager to join us."

The men stood panting, staring at each other, their eyes blazing with angry fire.

"Tom!"

Out of the darkness came a flurry of rustling damask as Kate flung herself on him. Middlemore's attention was distracted momentarily from his prey and Carew saw his chance. Pushing Middlemore to the ground, he lunged forward, and in an instant was on his horse and away.

Frantically, Kate struggled to untie the rope from Tom's hands. Her hot tears fell onto his face as she fought with the knots.

Tom looked up at John as he rubbed his chafed wrists. The groom was grim-faced and sweating.

"Back to the house. If we're quick we can stop them at the river."

Tom sprang to his feet, and all three of them ran back to the Hall, not knowing nor caring how or where they ran.

As they burst into the Great Hall, a terrible sight met their eyes. All was still, all was silent, except for one person. Lady Haswell stood weeping, ashen-faced and alone in the centre of the room, her guests staring at her in confusion. Some of her guests sneered and mouthed insults about their hostess. Others looked reproachfully down their noses at her. Not one went to her aid. Sir Richard was pinioned between two burly armed men that Tom had never seen before. In front of Sir Richard, his sword drawn and glinting was Sir Charles Gerard, the Sheriff. He gestured with his sword as Sir Richard attempted to free himself of his captors.

"Treason, sir. Treason—that's what this is. There was a priest here tonight, a guest at your feast, by God, hidden with your connivance, no doubt. Father John Stockton of Langford—he's led us a merry dance these past weeks. And all the time he was enjoying your hospitality and protection. Thank God for loyal men like Sir Jacob Carew. He knew his duty was to report your treason to me, and will soon be holding him prisoner."

Stockton was the priest? And Carew had turned informant on his own friends and betrayed them to Sir Charles? Tom curled his lips instinctively. Was there no limit to the man's disloyalty?

The tip of Gerard's sword pricked Sir Richard's throat. Tom's knees went weak and he clung to Middlemore lest he fall. Beside him, Kate whimpered in terror.

"And there's more, Haswell," continued the Sheriff. "Swords. Two boxes of them, and papers that tell of a plot to kill His Majesty King Henry and put the Papist Mary on the throne. Thanks once more to Sir Jacob's information, your plot has been foiled. By God's Wounds, you'll hang for this feeble web of treason. It's the Assizes at Lancaster for you. Take him away."

The two men holding Sir Richard dragged him towards the door. Lady Haswell screamed, her arms held outstretched beseechingly, pleading for mercy.

"No!" came a voice beside Tom. It was Middlemore. "No, you've got the wrong man. Ask the Constable. Ask Harry, he knows. And the boy, he's seen their wickedness."

The Sheriff turned to face the groom. "And who are you? Some legal expert, hmm? I don't think so. You're just the groom."

"No, sir. My name's Middlemore, sir." John's voice was deferential now.

"Middlemore? A Papist name, surely? And you think I've got the wrong man, do you? Well, sir, I'm damn sure I've got the right man, and no treacherous dog is going to tell me otherwise. Haswell's for Lancaster, and you'll follow if you don't keep your heretic mouth shut."

Gerard strutted to the door as Sir Richard was

132

dragged roughly away. He turned to face the shocked guests.

"The party's over—unless you all want to join him in the Castle dungeon? I bid you farewell."

He made a mocking bow to Lady Haswell and left abruptly.

A slow murmur arose, and the guests started to drift slowly to the door, not one of them daring to speak to their hostess, who had begun to moan uncontrollably. It was left to one of the servants to lead her away gently. Kate followed, sobbing.

Tom watched, trembling, as the last of the guests shuffled hurriedly out to their waiting horses. His worst fears had been fulfilled; Carew and his band of conspirators had got clean away, leaving his innocent father to take the blame. And now their closest friends, all with power and influence, had deserted them. From a room deep within the Hall, a tormented wailing echoed.

"Look at them," said Tom in disgust. "They were quite happy to eat our food, and now they can't even manage to say good-bye. We've certainly found out who our friends are."

As he unconsciously echoed Edward's words, Tom walked slowly to the entrance to the house. Middlemore followed and stood beside him. In the distance, he could see the dancing flames of the Midsummer bonfires dotting the hilltops. A jagged flash of lightning split the sky, and several moments later the thunder roared angrily. A soft pattering announced the long-threatened rain. Tom watched as the raindrops increased in intensity, causing the delicate petals of a red climbing rose to fall to the ground. A heavy tiredness took over his limbs and he leaned weakly against the door.

"John? Is that you?"

The gruff voice of Harry Wiswall broke the silence.

"Ay, it is. What news, Harry? Did you find them?" Middlemore's tone betrayed no glimmer of hope.

"Oh, we found them, that's for sure. Both of them were in a ditch over by Glebe's Corner—Hussey with his throat slit from ear to ear. And Stockton—stone dead. Poisoned, it looks like. But whether by his own hand, or that of another, I can't say."

Middlemore snorted, derisively.

"Well, I could, Harry. That wastrel Carew would stop at nothing. He's dangerous, and now he's on the run."

Tom stared at Harry. He could contain his loathing for Carew no longer.

"My father was fooled by these traitors—and Gerard was surely one of them. I saw him with Carew—and Stockton. He must have known he was a priest before he searched the house. They tricked my father with their spineless plot so Carew—Glover—could get this house and its land. That evil murderer may have escaped for the moment—but he'll be back to claim what he believes is his."

Stern-faced and with his jaw firmly set, Tom looked out over the neat, ordered gardens of Lower Myersford. A pale sheen of rain glistened on the lawns and the leaves of the low cut bushes trembled under the weight of the raindrops. In the corner of a window-frame a tiny spider scurried to make repairs to her web, damaged by the storm. Tom watched as the tiny, determined creature spun and worked her way along, repairing the broken threads of her labour.

"Tom."

Middlemore's voice resonated in the darkness. Tom turned to face him. The groom was gazing down at him, his eyes radiating warmth and kindness.

"The world's changing, Tom. Breaking up, melting into nothing, like the ice melts into the stream and is gone. You have to be the man now, to care for your mother and your sister. With your father gone, they need your protection." Middlemore put his arm round Tom's shoulders.

Yes, thought Tom. We all need protection—and my father, too. He needs me now, more than ever.

He looked up at Middlemore.

"Will you help me, John? Because as long as I have breath, I will fight for my father's freedom and good name. And to keep Myersford."

Middlemore's eyes narrowed and he looked keenly at Tom.

"Do you need to ask, Tom? I served your father and now I serve you."

Tom straightened his back to pull himself up to his full height. Behind him, a noise attracted his attention. He spun round and saw one of his father's servants hovering, awaiting instruction. Tom breathed in deeply and decisively.

"Lock up the house and make it secure. Arrange for someone to keep watch outside tonight, and make sure my mother is cared for. If Carew returns, we'll be waiting for him."

A heavy weight lay across Tom's chest and his eyes threatened to spill the tears he had held back for so long. His throat burned as he tried to speak.

"My thanks for your efforts, Master Constable. Now I must attend to my family."

Overhead, another flash of lightning lit the night sky, its angry fork of destruction streaking down to earth. For a brief second, Tom saw the Haswell estates stretching out into the valley, the foothills of the Pennines and the humble dwellings of the farm workers. And silhouetted against the brightness, small and insignificant now, he saw the outline of his innocent father receding into the distance as he was led away, flanked by his accusers, to face trial at Lancaster. Then the blackness of the night enveloped him like a shroud, and Tom could see him no more.